PROTECTING THE BILLIONAIRE

THE SHERBROOKES OF NEWPORT BOOK 7

CHRISTINA TETREAULT

Protecting The Billionaire, Copyright 2016 by Christina
Tetreault
Published by Christina Tetreault

Cover Model: Jon Eric Doliana II
Model Photos: Green Owl Photography
Cover design by: Leah Kaye Suttle
Editing: Hot Tree Editing

PRINT ISBN: 978-0-9971118-1-1

This book is dedicated to my grandfather, John Raimondo. Born and raised in the Federal Hill section of Providence, Rhode Island to Italian immigrants, he was the second of five children. He served in the Navy during World War II, and in 1951, he married my grandmother, Viola Gaucher. They moved to Pawtucket, Rhode Island, where he lived until his death in 1995. Many of Rock's expressions and personality traits I pulled from my grandfather, a man I have wonderful memories of and still miss.

This book is dedicated to my grandfather, John Raimondo. Born and raised in the Federal Hill section of Providence, Rhode Island to Italian immigrants, he was the second of five children. He served in the Navy during World War II, and in 1951, he married my grandmother, Viola Gaucher. They moved to Pawtucket, Rhode Island, where he lived until his death in 1995. Many of Rock's expressions and personality traits I pulled from my grandfather, a man I have wonderful memories of and still miss.

CHAPTER 1

"WHAT ARE YOU STILL DOING HERE?"

Allison turned her chair toward where her cousin and boss, Jake Sherbrooke, stood. She thought he'd already left for the night like everyone else in the office.

"I wanted to finish this up before the weekend. I'm almost done."

"Do you want me to wait for you?"

"Nope. I promise I'll leave as soon as I'm done with this paragraph." She'd been working on the grant proposal since the previous week. Once she finished this section, she'd have a preliminary draft to present to her cousin.

For a moment, Jake remained silent, his fingertips drumming on the top of another chair. "That's what you said Wednesday night and you ended up staying until nine."

He had her there. However, that hadn't been her intention. When she'd told him she planned on leaving soon, she'd meant it. Somehow she'd lost track of time, and before she realized it, her stomach was rumbling and her watch read nine. Tonight, she wouldn't let that happen.

"Cross my heart, I'll only stay another twenty minutes."

"Okay, but if you're late, it'll be your fault two pregnant

1

women have to wait for their dinners," Jake said as he pulled on his suit jacket. "You don't want to see Charlie when she's hungry these days."

She'd gone out with her cousin's wife three weeks ago, and it did seem as if Charlie's appetite had grown exponentially since reaching the end of her pregnancy. "Trent would never let me hear the end of it either if I showed up late." Allison turned back toward her computer screen. "So the sooner you leave, the sooner I'll be done."

"It's always nice talking to you too, cuz." Jake started toward the door. "See you soon."

Allison waited until he left before she went back to typing, the sound of her fingertips hitting the keyboard the only noise in the office. Both a Friday and St. Patrick's Day, the office had cleared out the moment five o'clock rolled around. Not that she blamed anyone. Who wanted to be stuck behind a desk on a Friday night, especially now that it remained light out longer and the weather had turned milder? Last year at this time, she would've locked her office door and left with everyone else. Not now.

Ever since she started at her cousin's foundation in February, she'd worked hard to prove to everyone that she deserved her position, that Jake hadn't simply hired her because they were related. While no one had come out and said anything to her, she'd gotten that impression from a few of the employees in the office. And maybe Jake had offered her the job first because he was her cousin and knew she'd been itching for a change. But he never would've offered it if he didn't believe she was qualified. The Falmouth Foundation meant too much to him, and from what she could tell, he only hired highly qualified individuals.

"And done." With enthusiasm, she stabbed the period key before she saved the document and closed the program. First thing Monday morning, she'd do a last read-through before she met with Jake to discuss the proposal. Assuming he had no changes, she'd get the final documents sent out next week.

Gathering up her things, she pushed in her chair and headed out. She had more than enough time to stop home and change before she met everyone for dinner.

A crisp, refreshing breeze washed over her as she walked to her car. If she were in Rhode Island right now, she'd probably still be wearing a winter jacket. However, mid-March in Virginia was proving to be much milder than in New England—not that she'd ever complain about that. She might have been born and raised in New England, but she never loved the cold winters. While she wouldn't call Virginia a tropical paradise, it was milder than what she was used to. In her opinion, the warmer climate was just another perk of moving away from Providence, and there were several. The first being she no longer bumped into her ex-boyfriend Charles every time she turned around.

Yep, that was a definite perk.

Too bad there were also several downsides to moving. Since she'd relocated to Alexandria, she hadn't seen her dad and stepmom much. Before the move, she visited with them on a regular basis. She also hadn't seen her brothers. She complained about the four of them, but she was close to all of them, especially Derek, her twin. He kept promising to come and visit, but so far he hadn't made it down. The next time they spoke, she'd have to give him a hard time about that.

Snap.

Allison stopped, the hair on the back of her neck standing up. Glancing around the parking lot, she looked for the source of the sound. A few cars remained parked down the far end of the lot, but otherwise she appeared to be alone.

"It was probably something in the street," she muttered as she pulled open her car door. She really needed to stop overreacting to every little sound she heard. Otherwise, she was going to drive herself crazy.

"Hi, Allison, I thought that was you," a male voice called out from behind her.

Even though she recognized the voice, her heart beat a mile a minute as she turned. "Josh. Hey. I thought everyone had cleared out of the building already." She'd spoken with Josh, a young lawyer who worked at the law firm on the second floor, and his boyfriend on numerous occasions. Both came across as friendly, easygoing men.

"Got halfway to my car and realized I left my phone in my desk. If you're interested, Robbie and I are heading over to Flannigan's Pub for their Saint Patrick's Day party. Join us."

She didn't doubt a night out with the two men would be a blast, and if she didn't already have plans, she'd consider Josh's offer. "Thanks for the invite, but I'm meeting my brother and his wife for dinner tonight. I'd love to get together some other time."

"I'm going to hold you to that. Have a great weekend. See you next week," Josh said before he turned and walked toward the far end of the lot and the few cars still parked there.

Alone once again, she wasted no time getting into her car and pulling out.

Thanks to the unusually light traffic for a Friday evening, Allison made it home in less than fifteen minutes, a rare feat. Before she even turned the car engine off, she used the tiny remote on her keychain and switched on the table lamp in the main foyer. She'd found the handy device on the Internet. Although it was advertised as the perfect way to turn on and off outside holiday lights, she found it great for switching on interior lights as well. She didn't know how the technology worked, but she appreciated it. Over the past few months, she'd come to hate walking into a dark house alone.

Unlocking the front door, she heard her phone chirp, an indication she had a text message. After punching in her alarm code, she glanced at her phone.

Just checking to make sure you left work.

Allison rolled her eyes and typed back a response to Jake. **Home now.**

Good. Trent called. Addie's brother is joining us tonight

too.

Her sister-in-law had four older brothers, although she'd only met one of them, so Jake's text message didn't tell her much, other than their party would now number six instead of five.

As she walked toward the stairs, she kicked off her shoes, something she'd dreamed about doing since lunchtime. Today had been the first time she'd worn the new pumps, and her feet ached so much even the idea of putting shoes back on made her cringe.

Which one? she typed back, not that it mattered. She liked meeting and getting to know new people.

Rock. He was at the wedding.

An image of the Marine she'd danced with at Trent's wedding popped up. She hadn't thought of him since. Her move and work kept her from thinking about anyone, but at the wedding, she'd had trouble keeping her eyes off him. Something about a man in a uniform captured her full attention. It also helped that Rock was handsome. Perhaps not movie star handsome like her brothers, but in that rugged 'I'll take care of the woman I love' sort of way. No woman who met Rock Raimono would soon forget him.

I remember. See you soon.

Dropping the phone on her nightstand, Allison went straight for her closet. Dinner tonight was at Siena, an upscale Italian restaurant. She'd visited the establishment twice since she'd moved to the area, and while the restaurant remained classy and customers never dared show up in jeans, her office attire would stick out, as would the cozy slippers she wished she could slip on.

She'd decided on an outfit before she even left for the office, so it took her little time to change and retouch her makeup. The house phone rang just as she recapped her mascara. No one she cared about ever called her landline. The only reason she even had it installed was to make her dad happy. He insisted it made sense to have a second method of communication just in case something ever happened to her cell phone. Rather than argue with him, she had the line installed and more or less forgot about it. Since then, she'd received only a handful of calls on the phone. A few people had called looking for someone named Misty. Allison assumed either Misty had the number prior to her, or the woman's number was similar. And three or four times she'd gotten calls for Nick's Pizza, whose number was only different by one digit.

Then there had been the one call she kept telling herself was a wrong number. About two weeks earlier, she'd gotten a call late at night. It had actually woken her up. When she answered though, no one said anything. Usually when people realized they had a wrong number, they said *something*. That caller had just hung up.

Tonight, she ignored the phone all together and started on her hair. Eventually, the line went silent. A few seconds later though, it started up again. "I need to switch off the ringer."

Once again ignoring the phone, she brushed out her hair and then pinned some back. Satisfied with the image in the mirror, she switched off the lights and made her way downstairs. She reached the kitchen when the phone started up again.

Slipping her purse over her shoulder, she picked up the receiver. If the caller wanted Nick's Pizza, she'd give them the right number. She called them enough herself that she had the number memorized. Besides, who was she to stand between a person and their dinner?

"Hello," she said, expecting to hear the caller say they'd like to place a delivery order. Instead, silence greeted her. Well, maybe not complete silence. She thought she heard breathing. "Hello," she repeated. Had the caller heard her voice and realized they had the wrong number?

No response came, but she did hear what sounded like traffic in the background.

Goose bumps formed on her arms, and she put the receiver

down. If the caller didn't intend to say anything, she wasn't going to keep saying hello. Turning the phone around, she switched off the ringer. When she got home, she'd do the same on the phone in her bedroom.

Leaving the lights in the kitchen on, she picked up her keys and headed out.

Fifteen minutes later, she pulled into a parking spot next to Jake's new SUV. While he still used his favorite toy—a brand new Lamborghini—when he was alone, he always used the SUV he'd purchased a few months ago when he and Charlie went out together. She assumed it was because Charlie now found it difficult to get in and out of the low sports car, but Jake told her it was more a safety issue. He figured if they ever got into an accident, Charlie would be much better protected in the large SUV. She'd always adored her cousin Jake, but when he told her that, it had endeared him to her even more.

"I'm meeting friends tonight. I believe they've already been seated," Allison told the hostess once she walked inside. "Jake and Charlie—"

"Yes, I seated them a few minutes ago. Please follow me, Miss Sherbrooke," the hostess said before Allison could even finish her sentence. The fact the woman knew whom she meant didn't surprise her. There was no mistaking the family resemblance; the eyes tended to be a dead giveaway. Not to mention, while Allison did her best to avoid the media, she still ended up on magazine covers from time to time. Thankfully, however, she didn't find herself there as often as her former playboy brother Trent and cousin Jake.

Following the hostess, she ignored the casual glances she received from the men seated at the cocktail bar as they passed by it.

She saw Jake stand before she reached the table, a good indication he saw her coming.

"Right on time," he said as he pulled out her chair and then waited for her to sit.

Allison accepted the menu from the hostess but looked at her cousin. "I promised I'd be here on time." She turned her attention to his wife. "Hi, Charlie. How are you feeling?"

Charlie patted her stomach and smiled. "Tired but good."

"She doesn't rest enough," Jake inserted with a frown.

"This one would have me in bed all day watching television and napping," Charlie replied, titling her head toward Jake. "He's driving me crazy."

Pressing her lips together, she glanced at Jake, who'd turned his attention to his wife. "You're thirty-six weeks pregnant. You shouldn't be doing rounds."

"And how many babies have you had?" Charlie asked.

Allison imagined her brother and his wife had been having similar conversations lately. At least the last time she'd spoken with Addie, Trent's wife, she'd complained that Trent kept telling her to rest more.

"It doesn't matter anyway. Yesterday was my last day at the hospital," Charlie said before Jake could offer a counterargument.

"Wow, this conversation sounds familiar," a female voice rang out from behind her.

Standing, Allison turned and hugged her new sister-in-law and smiled at her oldest brother.

"That's because Jake and I are right," Trent said as he pulled out a chair for his wife.

"I don't know what the world would do without the two of you wise men." Allison moved closer to Trent and hugged him too.

"Please don't encourage him. His head barely fits in the car now," Addie teased before she leaned toward Trent and kissed his cheek. "Rock texted me and he's on his way. He had to take care of something before he left the base."

HE'D PASSED by Siena numerous times since he'd been transferred to Quantico, but he'd never stopped in. It wasn't his type of place. He preferred more casual joints where he could get a decent burger or a good steak with a cold beer to wash it down. Restaurants with fancy dipping oil for your bread and wine lists longer than his arm didn't interest him. Even so, when Addie invited him to join her and her husband's family for dinner, he couldn't say no. He hadn't seen his sister since her wedding in January. While he was used to going long stretches between visits with his family, it didn't mean he liked it, so he took every opportunity he got to see them. She'd offered to meet him some other day while she was in the area if that worked better for him, but he'd declined. Not only did he want to visit with her, but he also wanted to spend some time with her husband. Addie could take care of herself, and she'd never take any crap from a guy. Still, the big brother in him needed to know Trent better. The guy was his baby sister's husband and the father of his future niece or nephew. Regardless of the fact that Trent was a billionaire, if he ever treated Addie poorly, he'd be getting a not-so-friendly visit from him.

Rock entered the restaurant and headed for the hostess station.

"Name and party size?" the hostess asked after greeting him.

"I'm meeting the Sherbrooke party. They should've already arrived."

Several of the conversations around him stopped. Addie admitted she was still getting used to being a Sherbrooke. He suspected it was because of moments like these.

The hostess smiled at him and reached for a menu. "Yes, Mr. Sherbrooke said they were expecting one more tonight. Please follow me."

Dismissing the busybodies in the waiting area, Rock followed the hostess past the cocktail bar, noting all the emergency exits and quickly taking stock of the customers they passed.

He spotted his sister and brother-in-law near the back wall, but before he reached them, Addie stood and rushed toward him.

"Rock." She threw her arms around him.

Normally, he'd hug her right back, but tonight he paused. When he'd seen her in January, Addie hadn't looked pregnant. Now she looked like she'd swallowed a basketball. The last pregnant woman he'd probably hugged had been his mom when she'd been expecting Addison. He didn't want to hurt her.

"I won't pop if you hug me," Addie said, her voice low so no one else heard her.

"I just wasn't sure I'd get my arms around ya." No way was he admitting he'd been nervous about hugging his own sister.

"I'm so glad I invited you tonight. You're always so full of compliments." She flicked the back of his neck and then kissed his cheek.

Trent stood and extended his hand when they approached the table. "Rock, I'm glad you could join us. You probably remember my cousin Jake and his wife Charlie." Trent gestured toward the couple across from him. "And my sister Allison."

He remembered everyone, especially Miss Allison Sherbrooke. He only danced with her once at Addie's wedding, but it had been enough to scorch the image of the woman into his brain. He'd never tell anyone, but since the wedding, Allison had made many appearances in his dreams.

"It's nice to see everyone again. Thanks for including me." He made eye contact with each member of the party before his gaze swung back for one extra glance at Allison. *Mannaggia*, Rock thought, using one of his dad's favorite Italian curses, one he'd adopted himself. The word itself didn't translate into English, but it fit the moment, because damn if she wasn't the hottest woman he'd ever met. He suspected she'd be making another X-rated appearance in his dreams tonight.

"Trent wants me to stop working," Addie said as the conversation at the table started back up again. "Charlie, you're a doctor. Can you please tell him it's not necessary. It's not like I'm climbing ladders and lifting heavy objects."

"What's wrong with wanting to make sure you get plenty of rest before the baby comes?" Trent asked.

"I tried to tell Charlie the same thing. She wouldn't listen to me either," Jake added, sounding annoyed.

Rock saw his sister and Charlie exchange a look he couldn't decipher, before Charlie said, "As long as Addie's healthy, there's no reason for her to stop working unless her doctor tells her to."

He could've told his brother-in-law that trying to convince Addie to do something was pointless. She had a mind of her own. Most days, he considered that a good thing.

"My mom worked the day she had me." Addie looked looking in his direction. "Right, Rock?"

"Doesn't mean you need to," Rock said. Their parents had been in a very different financial situation than Addie and her husband. His sister could never work again and it wouldn't adversely affect her or her family.

Trent looked at him and nodded. "See? Even your brother agrees with me."

"Thanks a lot, Rock." Addie gave him a dirty look before she turned back to her husband. "I never said I was going to work right to my due date, just until the end of April. The baby isn't due until June."

"Maybe we should change the subject," Allison said, entering the conversation. "Dad said you won't tell him if you're having a girl or a boy."

Now that he thought about it, Addie hadn't told him either. Then again, he hadn't asked.

"That's because we don't know," Trent answered.

"Seriously? How can you not want to know?" Allison asked.

"We want to be surprised," Trent answered.

"You do realize it makes it impossible to buy gifts when you don't know if they're for a girl or a boy, right?" Allison asked, looking at the two married couples.

"Only a couple more weeks before you know our surprise," Jake said.

"You don't know what you're having either?" Rock asked. Only a handful of his buddies had kids, but they'd all known what they were having in advance. He assumed most couples did.

Charlie shook her head, drawing Rock's attention to her clenched jaw. "We decided to wait," she replied, her knuckles turning white as she gripped her water glass.

"Are you okay, Charlie?" Trent asked, telling him his brother-in-law had also noticed something appeared wrong.

Jake didn't give Charlie a chance to answer. "You're not fine. What's wrong?"

"I'm—" The rest of her sentence didn't come. Instead, Charlie took in a sharp breath.

"Charlie?"

There was no missing the worry in Jake's voice.

"It might have been a contraction." Charlie pasted on the fakest smile he'd ever seen and released her grip on the glass. "Should we order an appetizer? The stuffed mushrooms here are delicious."

"Are you serious? When did they start?" Jake pulled the menu from his wife's hands, not that Rock blamed him. If the woman was in labor, whether or not to order an appetizer shouldn't be on her mind.

"About forty minutes ago, but I'm not convinced they're not Braxton Hicks contractions."

He had no idea what those were, but if the word contractions was at all involved, a restaurant seemed like the wrong place to be sitting.

"We're going to the hospital." Jake stood and pulled back his wife's chair.

"Jake, even if they are real, we both know it'll be hours before anything happens. If we go to the hospital now, they'll send us home."

"Trust me, they won't send us home." Jake reached for Charlie's hand when she didn't stand.

"We're not going to the hospital," Charlie said, her voice ringing with all the authority of a gunnery sergeant. "But if it'll make you feel better, we can—" she paused again and took in a deep breath; after slowly exhaling, she continued "—go home."

Jake gave his wife's arm a little tug, his expression revealing the fact he wanted to argue but knew it'd be pointless. "Fine. Let's go. Now."

"It was nice seeing you again, Rock." Charlie stood in no apparent rush, and Rock wondered if she was intentionally being slow to annoy her husband. Somehow, he could picture his sister doing the same thing to Trent when the time came. "Addison, Trent, I'll see you on Sunday at the fundraiser."

Rock doubted Jake would let his wife out of the house again unless it involved a trip to the hospital.

"Charlie." Jake tugged his wife's arm again and received a swat on the hand in return.

Across the table, Trent laughed. "You look a bit worked up there, Jake. Do you need a ride home, or can you handle it?"

"Just wait, Trent, until it's your turn."

Trent laughed again. "Let us know what happens."

Charlie nodded and allowed Jake to lead her away from the table and out of the dining room.

"I've never seen him so worked up," Allison said from next to him.

He wouldn't have pegged Jake Sherbrooke for the type to overreact and worry either. After all, he did run a disaster relief foundation. He'd expect someone who did that type of work to be cool and collected in an emergency situation.

"If he keeps it up and Charlie is in labor, she'll kick him out of the delivery room," Trent said, picking up his menu as a waiter approached their table.

Conversation at the table stopped long enough for everyone to place their dinner orders. Once the waiter walked away, Rock looked back at his sister. "How long are you and Trent staying down here?" Assuming it fit into his schedule, he'd like to see them again before they returned to Providence.

"Until—" Trent's ringing phone cut off his sister.

"It's Jake," Trent said as he pulled out his cell phone. "I bet he does need help getting home."

No one spoke as Trent answered the phone. "Keep us updated," Trent said after a few seconds. Then he put the phone back into his pocket and looked in Rock's direction. "We'll be here until Wednesday."

"Who cares?" Allison asked. "Why did Jake call? Is something wrong?"

Trent shrugged, and Rock suspected he was trying to annoy his younger sister. As an older brother himself, he knew how much fun that could be no matter your age.

"Nothing big. Charlie's water broke in the parking lot. They're headed to the hospital."

"That's terrible. Uncle Warren won't be around when this baby is born either," Allison said.

Rock almost laughed. To hear the President of the United States referred to as "Uncle Warren" just seemed wrong. After all, Warren Sherbrooke was one of the most powerful men in the world.

"He was in England when my cousin Callie had her son in September, and now he's in Turkey," Allison said, looking at him and explaining her comment. "He won't be back until Tuesday or Wednesday I think."

He felt for the man. He wouldn't be around when Addie gave birth in June. At least the President would see his new grandson or granddaughter in a matter of days. It'd be months before he got to meet his new niece or nephew.

Rock listened as the rest of the party discussed the upcoming fundraiser. He'd known it was the main reason Addie and Trent had traveled down to Virginia. He hadn't realized several other members of the Sherbrooke clan would also be present, including the President's youngest daughter and two of Trent's younger brothers.

"Hey, Allison, I think Charles just walked in."

Allison shifted in her seat, her arm bumping into his. "Trent, that's not funny."

Judging by the annoyance in Allison's voice, this Charles guy ranked low on her friend list.

"I'm not joking." Trent glanced back over at the entrance again. "And it must be him, because he's headed this way."

Rock heard Allison groan, and then she grabbed his hand, sending an electric shock across his skin. "Just play along," she said, and he wasn't sure if she was talking to him or everyone at the table.

A moment later, a well-dressed man in his early thirties stopped at their table. "Trent, what a coincidence running into you here," Charles said before he looked at Addie. "This must be your wife. Congratulations." He extended his hand toward Addie, and they exchanged the typical pleasantries before he looked in Rock and Allison's direction, his eyes momentarily glancing down at their clasped hand. "Allison, it's nice to see you again."

Allison squeezed his hand, perhaps as a reminder to play along, before she answered, "Hi, Charles. It's been awhile."

Rock imagined she was thinking it hadn't been long enough.

"I don't believe I've met your friend." Charles turned his narrowed eyes in his direction.

"This is my boyfriend. Rock, this is Charles Perkins, a friend of mine from Providence."

Oh, yeah. Charles hadn't liked her statement. If the guy's eyes narrowed anymore, they'd be closed.

Going with it, Rock nodded at the man. "Nice to meet you."

"Are you all down here for a visit?" Charles asked, and Rock thought he heard Allison groan.

"Uh, Trent and Addie are here for a fundraiser, but I work for the Falmouth Foundation in Alexandria now," Allison said.

Charles offered up a tightlipped smile. "Really. I didn't know you took a position there."

Bullshit. If Rock was good at one thing, it was smelling BS a mile away.

"Then I guess I'll see you all at the fundraiser."

"You'll be there?" Allison asked, her voice a few octaves higher than normal.

The man's smile widened, revealing his unnaturally white teeth. "My friend Daniel told me about it. He and his wife are going, and it's a good cause, so I bought a ticket as well. That's actually why I'm here tonight. We're meeting for dinner." Charles pointed at a couple seated across the dining room. "It was nice seeing everyone tonight. I'm sure I'll see you all on Sunday."

He watched Mr. Teeth—Rock thought the name fit him—walk toward his friends and waited for Allison to release his hand.

"Something you want to share, Allison? I didn't know Rock here was your boyfriend," Trent said with a chuckle, and Rock knew the guy was trying to get under his sister's skin.

Allison rolled her eyes, making her appear more like an annoyed younger sister rather than the beautiful socialite she was. "Knock it off. I was afraid he'd ask me out again. Since we broke up, he does it every time we run into each other. That's one of the reasons I was anxious to move. I was always running into him in Providence. It drove me nuts."

Yep, an ex-boyfriend. Sounded like the guy couldn't move on, not that Rock blamed him. He imagined most guys would hate getting the boot from a woman like Allison Sherbrooke. From the little Addie had told him about her, she was not only beautiful, but also smart and genuinely nice. Not to mention she came from a powerful family.

Perhaps realizing she still held his hand, she released it and reached for her water glass instead. "Unfortunately, he still calls every so often."

"Looks like we'll be seeing you on Sunday night, Rock. I hope you didn't have any other plans."

Allison's sharp intake of breath indicated she understood her brother's comment. It took Rock a second longer to unravel Trent's meaning.

"Shoot. I didn't think of that," Allison said.

Out of the corner of his eye, he saw her bite down on her lip. How many times since the wedding had he dreamed about her pleasuring his body with those lips? The image of her doing that now surfaced, and Rock was damn glad he was sitting down with a napkin covering his lap.

"Would you mind coming with me Sunday night?" She touched his arm as she spoke, sending a bolt of desire straight to his crotch.

He'd come tonight so he could visit with his sister and get to know his brother-in-law, not so he could get roped into attending some la-di-da dinner surrounded by people he had no desire to hang around.

Her fingers curled around his wrist. "If you can't, I understand."

Say no. He'd fit in at an event like the fundraiser about as well as a bull in a china shop. The anxiety in Allison's voice kept the two-letter word from coming and turned on his protective instincts. "Give me the time and location and I'll be there."

Two hours later, Rock followed everyone outside, somewhat bummed the evening was over. With the exception of now being stuck playing the role of a fake boyfriend, he'd enjoyed spending time with his sister, her husband, and her sister-in-law.

"Allison, where did you park?" Trent asked.

"Down near the lot entrance."

"I'll walk you. We're parked right here." He pointed to a silver Mercedes, used his key remote to unlock it, and then pulled open the door for Addie.

His sister had mentioned Trent always did that for her. She'd told him in the beginning it had taken a lot of getting used to.

Now, she no longer thought about it. She'd even recommended he start doing it when he took a woman out. As if the woman he dated would care either way.

"Don't worry about it. I'll be fine. There are plenty of lights around. Take Addie back to Jake's. She looks tired."

Anticipating Trent's response, Rock spoke before his brother-in-law had the chance. "I'll walk Allison to her car. I parked down there too."

"Thanks, Rock. I appreciate it," Trent said as he closed the passenger side door and walked around the car. "I'll see you both Sunday night."

He'd already suspected Addie was in good hands with Trent. However, Trent's treatment of Addie all night and the fact he didn't want his own sister walking in a parking lot alone verified Rock's beliefs. "See ya then."

Inside during dinner, he'd done more listening than actual talking. Now that it was only the two of them, Rock didn't know what to say. Judging from their vastly different backgrounds, they wouldn't have much in common, and he'd rather shoot himself in the foot than ask her about the weather.

Allison saved him from having to speak first. "Thanks again for agreeing to come Sunday. If I'd known Charles would be at the fundraiser, I never would've said we're dating. He doesn't seem to get the message. I thought maybe telling him I had a boyfriend would help."

"Don't worry about it."

"Still, I owe you one." She stopped under one of the parking lot lights. "This is me." She pointed over her shoulder. "If you have trouble finding my house or change your mind, call me." She'd given him her cell number and address before they walked outside. Both were now stored in his smartphone.

Rock looked at the car behind her. One side of its front end was slightly higher than the other. "You've got a flat."

"What? Again?"

Allison turned, giving him the opportunity to once again

appreciate the view she provided. Seated inside the restaurant, he'd been denied seeing the sexy legs her skirt revealed. Outside under the light with her back to him, however, he could admire all he wanted. Her legs weren't the only things he admired. His palms itched to reach out and cup her shapely ass.

"I had a flat tire last week too." She dropped her shoulder bag on the hood and searched inside. "I'll call the auto club and have them come change it."

He'd have it changed and she'd be home before the club got anyone there. "Don't bother. I got it. Pop the trunk."

She pulled her phone out and looked at him. "You'll get your clothes dirty. It won't take them that long to get here, and you don't have to stay. I promise to sit in the car with the doors locked and wait."

"Allison, pop the trunk. I'm not leaving ya here to wait." He'd only heard everyone address her by her full name, yet in his head it didn't fit. She struck him more as an Ally. When she didn't comply right away, he took the key remote from her hand and unlocked the trunk himself. "It'll only take me a few minutes."

A gentle mist started up and sprayed his face as he put the spare tire on the ground near the flat one. The weather forecast predicted light showers through most of the night and ending sometime after midnight. He had no complaints with that. He'd never been a big fan of running in the rain, and he planned to meet his buddy Brayden for a run at five o'clock in the morning. Walking past the driver side door on his way back to the trunk, he pulled it open. "Why don't ya sit inside so ya don't get wet?"

"It's just mist. I'm fine."

Rock grabbed the car jack and walked past her again. If she wanted to stand outside and get wet, that was her business. Sliding the jack under the car, he raised it. The click of heels walking across pavement had him glancing in Allison's direction for a brief second before he refocused on his task.

Mannaggia, that woman shouldn't go out without her legs

covered. They could stop a man dead in his tracks and make him beg for a minute or two of her time.

Once he had the car high enough, he grabbed the cross wrench on the ground and attacked the nuts on the tire. The sooner he finished, the sooner he got them both out of here.

"You make it look easy." She bent down and looked over his shoulder, her breath warming the back of his neck and her subtle perfume teasing him.

"It is. My sister could've handled this." He, along with his older brothers and dad, had made sure their baby sister knew how to take care of herself, and that had included minor repairs to her car.

Once he loosened all the nuts, he cranked the jack up more so the tire lifted off the ground, and then he pulled off the flat. "Looks like you drove over a nail." He pointed to the nail head embedded in the rubber tread.

"I did something similar last week, but the mechanic only found the hole."

Her breath on his neck reminded him just how close she remained. The memory of the last dream he'd had that she starred in resurfaced, and he forced the memory of the night his mutt Baxter got sprayed by a skunk up instead. If anything could kill a guy's growing erection, it was the smell of a skunk, or in this case the memory of the odor.

Grabbing the spare tire, he mounted it on the car and worked as fast as possible to get it secured in place. He needed to get away from Allison and her sexy legs. "Good to go." He carried the flat tire and jack back to the trunk.

"You were right." Allison stood leaning against the driver side door and watching him. "If I'd called the auto club, I'd still be waiting. Last week, it took them an hour to get to me. Looks like I owe you two favors now."

Man, he knew just how he'd like to collect those favors too. Too bad those weren't the type of favors she had in mind.

CHAPTER 2

WHO THE HELL IS THAT? She'd arrived alone and didn't have a boyfriend. So who was the bastard changing her tire? He'd been standing out here for the past hour waiting for her. Now, some ass with more muscles than brains had her attention. That wasn't how things were supposed to be. He should have her attention, not anyone else.

Across the lot, the SOB who'd changed Allison's tire closed the trunk. After exchanging a few words, Allison got into her car. He'd missed out on an opportunity tonight, but there would be others. He'd make sure of it.

Turning the key in the ignition, he pulled out. He knew the route Allison would take home. He'd just follow and make sure she arrived there safely and, more importantly, alone. She hadn't shown the dude who'd changed her tire any affection, but he also hadn't been a stranger. She'd known him. Nothing and no one was going to come between them. He'd make sure of that. Allison might not realize it yet, but she belonged with him. No one loved her as much as he did. Soon, she'd know the truth. And if anyone tried to get between them, he'd do what he had to.

CHAPTER 3

SHE'D SKIPPED the flowers in the gift shop downstairs and grabbed a baby blue teddy bear and a balloon instead. Now, seeing Charlie's hospital room, she was glad she'd opted for the bear. Vases filled with flowers overwhelmed the small room, making it smell more like a greenhouse than a hospital room. In her opinion, it was a huge improvement. She'd never liked the industrial cleaner smell that seemed to cling to every hospital or doctor's office she'd ever stepped into. The smell of flowers, on the other hand, she adored.

Stopping next to the bed, she hugged Charlie, who looked wiped out but happy. "Did you throw my cousin out?"

"I've considered it a time or two," she said with a smile as she accepted the bear. "But no, he just went to the cafeteria. You know him and coffee."

Oh, she knew all about Jake's obsession with coffee. Other than her cousin, she'd never known anyone who had started drinking the stuff at the age of twelve. From what Jake had told her, Charlie was just as bad, and it had been difficult for her to give it up when she became pregnant.

"Is he sleeping?" From where she stood, she could only see the back of the newest Sherbrooke member.

Charlie nodded as she placed a hand on her son's back. "For the moment. It won't last. He eats almost every hour on the hour."

"Sounds a lot like Jake." Her cousin was and always had been a bottomless pit when it came to food. How the guy never gained weight amazed her.

"You know my husband well." Charlie managed to get the words out right before a yawn escaped.

Unable to help herself, Allison walked around to the bassinet for a better look at Garret. Sound asleep, he looked like the most peaceful baby on Earth, with a full head of light blond hair and tiny fingers, which were curled up in a fist. "He's beautiful. Did you decide on a middle name?" When Jake called and announced they'd had a boy, he'd told her they were still going back and forth on a middle name.

"Ruari, after Ma's dad."

"Garret Ruari Sherbrooke. Sounds nice together," Allison said, watching the little bundle move but not wake up. "Garret? Isn't that Aunt Elizabeth's father's name?" She'd heard the name somewhere before, but she wasn't positive where.

"No, it's Elizabeth's grandfather's name. So Jake's great grandfather. Some of Jake's other ancestors have it too. I guess it was originally a surname and someone decided to use as a first name generations ago. Believe it or not, when we told Elizabeth his name yesterday, she cried."

She'd only seen her Aunt Elizabeth cry a handful of times. If a simple name made her cry, it must mean a great deal to her. "Has she been in today too?"

"She promised to stop in later this afternoon before the fundraiser."

She'd make sure she was gone before then. While she loved her aunt, she didn't love the secret service agents who accompanied her everywhere. Not that she had anything against them personally. It was just the fact that they were around. Ever since her Uncle Warren first decided to run for president, the agents had become a permanent part of his life as well as his wife's, and, to some extent, his children's lives. While Jake told them to take a hike not long after Uncle Warren took office, her cousin Sara still had agents assigned to her. Whenever they went out together, the agents weren't far behind, making her grateful her Uncle Warren and not her father resided in the White House.

Unfortunately, secret service agents would be at the fundraiser tonight. Nothing under the sun would keep Aunt Elizabeth from a fundraiser supporting Jake's foundation.

Charlie readjusted her position in bed and winced but didn't complain. "Ma and Sean will be back later today too and they'll stay a while. They're leaving on Monday, so Sean will probably have to drag Ma out of here tonight."

She'd only met Charlie's mother and brother once, but they'd both seemed nice and Jake only said good things about them. "Garret's her first grandchild, right?"

"Yeah, but I don't think she'll have to wait long for another. My brother is getting married this summer and his fiancée is anxious to start a family." A cry came from the bassinet and Charlie reached in for her son. "Since Ma and Sean will be here tonight, I'm trying to convince Jake to at least stop in the fundraiser and make an appearance."

"And I told you I'd think about it." Jake entered the room carrying a tray of food. "If I'm not there, Allison will be. She can give my speech. She helped me write it anyway." After putting down the tray, he hugged her before he looked at Charlie. "They didn't have any french fries, so I got you onion rings."

Allison's heart melted as she watched her cousin first kiss his wife's cheek and then place a kiss on his son's head. "And just about everything else in the cafeteria," Allison joked, eyeing the tray Jake carried in.

"Only about half of what's in the cafeteria is edible, and you never know which items that'll be. It's safer to grab a little of everything and save yourself a trip back."

Interesting logic, but if it worked for him, who was she to argue?

"I heard Rock's accompanying you tonight." Jake took his coffee off the tray before anything else and took a sip.

Charlie looked up at her as she covered her shoulder and chest so Garret could nurse. "Addie's brother at the restaurant Friday night? How did that happen?"

Trent had a big mouth. Her sister-in-law wouldn't have told Jake that little bit of news. "Not long after you two left, Charles walked in and saw us. I lied and said Rock was my boyfriend. Now he expects to see us together at the fundraiser."

"Why did you tell him that?" Jake asked, releasing his coffee long enough to rip open a bag of potato chips.

"I didn't want him asking me out again. I've told him a bunch of times I'm not interested, but he doesn't get the message. I thought, if he believed I have a boyfriend, he'd leave me alone. If I'd known he bought a ticket to the fundraiser, I wouldn't have said anything." Allison grabbed a potato chip from the bag her cousin held toward her. "And it's not like I can skip it. Rock was nice enough to agree to go when I asked him."

"How long ago did you and Charles break up?" Charlie asked.

"Some time before Halloween, so five or six months ago. And he's been pestering me ever since." She wondered why she'd dated him for so long in the first place.

Jake paused between bites of his sandwich to speak. "And he's still bugging you? Most guys would've gotten the hint by now."

If the tables were reversed, she would've gotten the hint a long time ago. Then again, Charles was unique. "Maybe seeing me with someone else will be that final push he needs to get it through his thick head."

≈

25

AFTER SLIPPING on the new gown she'd purchased for the fundraiser, Allison stepped in front of the mirror. With the exception of the frown reflecting back at her, she liked what she saw. Prior to two nights ago, she'd been looking forward to the evening. In general, she loved parties and fundraisers. She enjoyed the interaction with people and simply found it fun to put on a gorgeous dress and go out. Unfortunately, Charles's announcement Friday killed her enthusiasm for tonight's event. She'd even tried to come up with a good excuse her conscious would accept to get her out of it. Plenty of other Sherbrookes would be in attendance. In the end though, she knew she couldn't skip this one. When she'd left the hospital, Jake had still been up in the air about attending, even though Charlie kept insisting he should go. Allison knew he didn't want to leave his wife and new son's side, even if only for a short time. If Jake didn't attend, she more or less became the foundation's official representative tonight.

On the bright side, at least she wouldn't be showing up alone, which meant Charles wouldn't pester her all night like he had at the Browns' Christmas party. That night, he'd hung around her so much several people asked her later if they'd gotten back together. Tonight though, with Addie's brother by her side, Charles would keep his distance. Charles was an intelligent, power-driven man, but more or less a wimp. He wouldn't risk making Rock angry by hitting on his girlfriend.

At the thought of Rock, Allison's reflection smiled back at her. In the past, she'd dated sophisticated, professional men. Men who had attended Ivy League universities and who now spent their days putting more money in their already impressive bank accounts—not that there was anything wrong with that. The same description more or less fit her brothers too. However, since she'd started work with the Falmouth Foundation, she found herself bored with those types of men. Perhaps that explained why she was eager to see Rock again tonight. She didn't know much about him, but she looked forward to learning more.

Allison added all she could fit into her matching clutch before she headed downstairs. She'd offered to meet Rock at his apartment, but he insisted he'd pick her up. He claimed it made more sense because her townhouse in Alexandria was closer to the Keystone Hotel in DC than his apartment in Dumfries. She suspected there was more to it than simple proximity. Rock didn't strike her as the type of guy to let a woman pick him up for an evening out. In the long run, it didn't matter as long as she reached the fundraiser on time.

Door chimes echoed through the house as she came down the front stairs into the foyer. Glancing out the window before she opened the door, her belly did a little shimmy when she spotted Rock outside.

Holy moly. She'd forgotten just how panty-melting gorgeous he looked in his full Marine dress uniform. Without a doubt, tonight he'd catch the eye of more than one female in attendance.

"Please come in," she said after opening the door.

"Sorry for being late."

Late? She'd told him six and the wall clock read six now. "You're right on time."

Rock pointed to the large watch on his left wrist. "It's five minutes past."

Allison pressed her lips together. The only other alternative was to laugh. He appeared dead serious, and she suspected he'd find laughter an insult. "We still have plenty of time anyway. Let me grab my keys and wrap, and then we can go."

Rock gave her a stiff nod, and she turned away before he caught her smile. Friday night, he hadn't come across as quite so serious. Was that because then his sister had been around and he'd been more relaxed, or did it have something to do with the uniform? Either way, she hoped he loosened up a little as the night went on. The main goal of the fundraiser was to raise money; however, it was still a party. Parties were for having fun.

As always, several cars lined the street out front. The only downside to living where she did, most of the residents had to park on the street. Only a few of the historic townhomes had driveways, and even those that did could only fit one car. Even with the flaw, she hadn't been able to pass up the historic three-bedroom townhouse built in 1850 when she'd gone house hunting in January.

"I'm parked over here," Rock said, pointing in the direction of the utility pole where two vehicles, a big black pickup truck and a white two-door sedan, were parked. She'd never noticed either vehicle in the area before, but something told her the pickup belonged to Rock.

When he pulled out his car remote and the taillights of the pickup blinked, she knew she'd guessed right. Allison eyed the distance from the ground to the truck door. If she had on pants, she could climb up without too much difficulty. However, unless Rock picked her up, she saw no way for her to get inside tonight and maintain any dignity. They'd have to take her car.

Rock opened the passenger side door and waited, reminding her a bit of the Marines she'd walked past when she visited Uncle Warren at the White House. Much like those men, Rock's posture was perfect and his face was devoid of any emotion. Yep, the man really needed to loosen up a little bit if he was going to have any fun tonight.

"We can't take your truck tonight. Do you mind if we take my car instead?"

Rock's jaw moved a fraction of an inch, or she thought it did.

"There's no way I can get in wearing this dress." She gestured down to the narrow skirt, which reached her ankles, and his eyes followed her hand.

Closing the door, he nodded. "I didn't consider that."

Allison shrugged, her wrap slipping down her shoulder. Before she could pull it back up, the silk brushed against her skin as he moved it for her. Surprised by his thoughtfulness, she smiled at him. "This gown might make it difficult for me to drive. Do you mind?" She held the keys out toward him. She'd driven in similar gowns before, so she could do it, but if she didn't have to, all the better.

"What's the best way to reach the George Washington Parkway from here?" he asked, starting up the car once he got behind the wheel.

Making herself comfortable, she reached out and turned on the heated seat. The temperatures had stayed in the low 60s for much of the day, but they were dropping fast and the leather seat was cold. "Take a right out of the driveway and head straight. Then take your first left. That will take us straight to the parkway."

With another stiff nod, Rock backed out of the driveway and headed down Cameron Street. Several seconds ticked by and she kept waiting for him to say something. Even if he only commented on the weather. Instead, he remained tightlipped and silent as he followed her directions. She'd never cared much for silence. Even when she was alone at home, she liked some kind of background noise, whether it came from the stereo or the television. She guessed after growing up in a house with four brothers silence was just too foreign to her.

"Did you get to see Addie and Trent yesterday?" Since it didn't look like he planned to say much, she better; otherwise, this would be one heck of a quiet ride.

"Yeah, they came by."

Allison kept a steady conversation all the way into the city. At first, Rock only answered the questions she put out there. By the time they reached the Keystone Hotel, though, he'd started to offer up a little more information and even ask a few impersonal questions of his own. It was a start anyway.

"This is my favorite hotel in DC," Allison said once they left her car with the valet. "From the ballroom on the top floor, you get an incredible view of the city."

Rock took her arm as they passed through the glass doors and into the lobby. "There's a hotel in Providence like that."

"Do you mean the Bellevue?"

"Yeah, my high school senior prom was held there."

"I've been there a few times. This hotel is similar. I think they were built around the same time, although I like this one a little more." The elevator doors opened and together they stepped inside. "Most people don't know this, but the entire third floor is a private apartment. It has its own elevator and everything. Emerson Mulligan, the original owner who built the hotel, set it up for his mistress and their son. He ran his entire hotel chain from the offices on the second floor but lived in Alexandria with his wife and daughters. Supposedly, Mulligan's wife never found out about his mistress or son."

"Someone found out or ya wouldn't know," he said, once again pronouncing the you in the sentence so it sounded like it ended in an *a* instead. She'd noticed he often did the same thing two nights ago too.

"Mulligan died several years after his wife and left most of his money and multiple homes to his daughters, but he left the company to his son. People who knew Emerson Mulligan say he didn't believe women belong in business. His son didn't want anything to do with the company and sold it to my grandfather."

The elevator doors opened, revealing a sight she'd seen numerous times. Women, many of whom she knew, chatted with each other, their jewelry glittering under the lights. Men dressed in tuxedos stood around, probably discussing politics or the latest stock market numbers. At any other time, she'd jump in the foray, complimenting the women on their designer dresses and smiling at the men as they asked about her father or one of her uncles. Tonight, she glanced at her date instead and again kicked herself for lying to Charles in the first place. Even her brothers didn't love these things and they knew most of the people in attendance. Rock was going to be bored to death tonight.

Although many people mingled in the lobby area, most had already made their way into the ballroom, and Allison scanned the room for any of her brothers or cousins. Of all the guests there, she assumed Rock would be most comfortable around them. Right away she spotted Trent and Addie at one of the large round tables. "Trent and Addie are sitting over by the window. Let's join them."

Several other acquaintances greeted her as they crossed the room, but thankfully none seemed interested in long conversations at the moment. At least, not until they passed by Tasha Marshall, a woman a few years younger than her whom she'd known for as long as she could remember.

"Allison," Tasha called out as she and Rock passed near her table.

For a second, she considered whether or not she could pretend she hadn't heard Tasha and keep on walking. Over the years, they'd seen each other at countless events. She'd even attended Trent's wedding with the rest of her family. However, Allison never sought her out for conversations. It wasn't that she hated Tasha, but rather just found her rather annoying and a bit empty headed.

Unfortunately, both her mom and dad had drilled too many manners into her, and Allison stopped alongside Tasha's table. "Hi, Tasha. Thank you for coming tonight."

"Mother and Father asked me to join them," Tasha answered. "I didn't know you would be here."

"I work for the foundation."

"Really? So you live down here now? When did you move?" Tasha's eyes kept darting in Rock's direction, confirming her earlier belief that he was going to catch the eye of many women.

Before Allison provided an answer, Tasha gave Rock her full attention. "You look familiar. Have we met before?"

She'd seen the same glint in Tasha's eye before when she'd looked at her brothers and cousins. "Rock was at Trent's wedding."

Tasha's smile grew a little wider. "That's right. You were in the wedding party. You're Addie's brother." She looked at Allison again. "I thought you had gotten back together with Charles. He talks about you all the time."

"No, Charles and I are just friends." Reaching for Rock's hand, she leaned closer to him, and continued, "If you'll excuse us, my brother is waiting."

Tasha glanced over her shoulder and Trent waved in their direction. "Sure. Rock, it was nice meeting you."

"You too," he replied, his deep, sexy, late-night DJ voice kicking her pulse up for a moment.

"Let's chat again tonight, Allison. I know my parents would like to say hi to you and they should be here soon."

She'd rather avoid any further conversation with Tasha, but realized the probability of that was low, especially if Tasha's parents were in attendance. She genuinely liked Richard Marshall and his wife, who were close friends of both her dad and Uncle Warren. "I'll stop back after dinner." She wouldn't drag poor Rock over again. As it was, she suspected Tasha would be seeking him out later.

Rock watched Allison walk toward the First Lady's table. His date for the evening was the President and First Lady's niece. *Talk about a friggin' head scratcher for you.*

"You should ask her out for dinner or something," Addie whispered, interrupting his thorough visual inspection of Allison's ass. "You haven't stopped staring at her all night."

If his sister had caught him staring, he wouldn't deny it. "Not happening."

Stopping near her aunt, Allison pulled out a chair between the First Lady and another man he didn't recognize. After giving her aunt a kiss and hug, she did the same thing to the man on her right. *Lucky SOB.*

"That's only AJ. He's Elizabeth's nephew from England," she said, her voice still low as she patted his hand.

His sister referred to the First Lady of the United States as if she were talking about a neighbor down the street. "Thanks for the family tree lesson."

"I'm serious. You should ask Allison out sometime. I think you'd have fun together."

The man his sister called AJ said something that made Allison's head fall back as she laughed, and he pictured himself kissing all the pale skin exposed by her low-cut dress. He'd touched her arm earlier tonight, so he already knew how soft her skin was. Now he'd give almost anything to know how it tasted against his lips.

"Already told ya. Not happening."

"When was the last time you went on a date?"

Addie could switch tactics all she wanted; it wouldn't change his mind. A woman like Allison Sherbrooke didn't date men like him. "Last month."

"I didn't ask when you last slept with a woman. How long has it been since you went out with someone you'd consider being in a real relationship with? You know, the kind you take to meet Mom and Dad?"

His sister knew him too well. Someday, he wanted what she had; he just hadn't had much luck finding it. Instead, he found women who wanted to change him into some nine-to-five, suit-wearing chump who got manicures. Or worse. He got involved with Corey, the first and only woman he'd thought might be the one, at least until he returned from one of his deployments. Evidently, no sooner had his boots touched down in Afghanistan and she started sleeping around. Of course she'd had an excuse. She claimed she'd been bored and missed him. She argued that none of those men had meant anything. He said *arrivederci*, as well as a few curses, and never looked back. That had been almost two years ago. Since then, he'd taken finding *the one* off the table and focused on other things.

"Just because I find her sexy doesn't mean what your talking about could ever exist between us. Did you forget she calls POTUS, Uncle Warren?"

"So does Trent."

He hated when his sister was right.

Addie poked him in the arm. "Don't even think about saying that's different."

His baby sister was getting quick. "It is."

Across the room, Allison gave the First Lady another hug before she stood. After saying something to the other people seated, she turned and walked in his direction, the movement of her hips and ass a red flag drawing the attention of every male present.

"Think about it. I've seen her looking at you tonight. She'd say yes if you asked her."

It panged him to do it, but Rock looked away from Allison and at his sister instead. "Let. It. Go."

Like a good annoyed little sister, Addie rolled her eyes and sighed. "Poor Trent. He looks miserable over there. I should go and save him."

His brother-in-law looked as though he was about to face a firing squad as he spoke with an older gentleman. "Looks like he just got reinforcements." He watched a couple join Trent.

"That's Trent's cousin Sara and her fiancé Christopher. They were at the wedding."

He'd recognized the woman. After all, she was the President's youngest daughter. Not to mention, there was no mistaking her for a Sherbrooke. Yet he couldn't honestly say whether or not he'd spoken with her back in January. Other than Allison, all the Sherbrookes he'd met that night had blended into one fuzzy memory.

Rock stored the information and went back to a more enjoyable activity—watching Allison walk back, envious of the damn dress she wore and the fact it got to cling to her body the way he dreamed about doing.

"Sorry I was gone so long." Allison slipped back into her seat, and a subtle floral fragrance teased him. "I haven't seen AJ in a long time. He doesn't visit the U.S. much. He's not a big fan of the long flight."

"Don't worry about it. I kept my brother company for you," Addie said.

"Looks like Senator Clark cornered Trent and Sara," Allison said.

He should have known the guy with his brother-in-law was a senator or congressman. This was DC.

"Nah, he trapped Trent. Sara and Christopher went over to rescue him," Addie joked as Trent shook hands with the senator and walked away, leaving his cousin and her fiancé behind.

"The older Senator Clark gets, the more he talks." Trent joined them again and immediately kissed his wife.

Rock couldn't deny that Trent constantly showered Addie with affection no matter the time or place.

"Allison, I saw Charles sitting with the Marshalls when I passed by them. I didn't realize they knew each other," Trent said.

He'd expected Mr. Teeth—he couldn't stop thinking of him that way—to seek them out tonight, yet they'd made it through dinner without a visit from him.

"Mrs. Marshall is good friends with his mom. On our first date, he took me to a 4th of July party at the Marshalls' home in the Hamptons."

The woman attended parties in the Hamptons, and Addie wanted him to ask her out. Yeah, that wouldn't end well.

"In case you didn't notice, he's headed this way," Trent said.

He assumed everyone at the table heard Allison's groan.

"Do you want to dance?" Rock dropped the question, and two pairs of eyes looked at him. Unless left with no other option, he stayed away from dance floors.

"Fantastic idea." Allison half led, half dragged him past Charles and onto the dance floor.

They'd danced once at the wedding. That night, she'd kept both her hands on his shoulders and maintained a polite distance away from him. Tonight, she pressed her body into him, her breasts crushed against his chest, and put her arms around his neck. While his head knew it was all an act, his body didn't. Unable to do anything about his growing arousal, he put his arms around her and went with it.

"Is he looking this way?" she said near his ear, her breath a sensual whisper against his skin.

More like sending death threats with his eyes. "Yep."

She wiggled closer, something he'd thought impossible. "Put your hands on my butt."

"What?" He didn't do high society, but groping a woman like Allison at this kind of event seemed like a no-no.

"Put your hands lower, like a real boyfriend would."

He'd wanted to touch her ass all night, and now she'd given him the green light. *Oorah.* Rock dropped his hands and almost groaned. He'd expected her ass to be firm. He hadn't expected it to fit perfectly in his hands. Behind his fly, his erection grew, pressing against the front of his pants. Under no circumstances could she miss it.

He moved them in time to the music, eventually turning them, making it impossible for him to see Charles any longer.

"He said something to Trent and now he's walking back toward the exit," Allison whispered near his ear.

Rock waited, expecting Allison to put a little breathing room between them now. If Mr. Teeth had left, then they no longer needed to pretend. Instead, she leaned her head against his shoulder.

I should move my hands. Deep down, he recognized it was the right thing to do. They'd done their little acting stint. Her ex was gone, at least for the moment. His hands should move up to her waist. Knowing and doing were two completely different things. *You don't get your hands on a perfect ass like this every-day,* his erection reminded him as the song continued and her body moved against his. Hell, it was likely he'd never had his hands on a woman as sexy as Allison before and wouldn't again. Since she'd given him permission and she wasn't complaining, why should he deny himself a few moments of pleasure?

When the final chorus of the song ended, Rock led her back to their table, where Trent sat alone.

"Very convincing out there." Trent's arched eyebrow and expression suggested he knew how much Rock enjoyed having Allison pressed up against him. "I doubt Charles will be calling you again," Trent said, turning his attention back to his sister.

At least their little dance had done something besides give him a boner he didn't see going away any time soon.

"I can hope," Allison answered, sitting back down again. "Where did Addie go?"

"She and Sara went to talk to Aunt Elizabeth."

Two hours later, Rock pulled into Allison's driveway, still aroused from the single dance they'd shared. If his body didn't cool off by the time he got back to his apartment, he'd be hitting the shower.

"Thank you for coming tonight." She touched his arm as they walked toward her front door. "I hope it wasn't too boring for you."

He'd certainly found himself in worse places; however, if tonight's fundraiser remained the last high-society event he ever attended, he'd be okay with that. "Not a problem. I hope your ex bought it."

"It's not too late. Would you like to stay and have some coffee?" Allison asked as she opened the door and stopped. "The alarm's not on," she said before he could answer, "and I thought I turned off all the lights upstairs."

Bright light streamed out of a room on the second floor. When he'd picked her up, he hadn't looked at anything but her, so he was the wrong guy to ask. "Maybe you forgot it." His mom periodically forgot to set the alarm system his dad had installed.

She glanced around again before she looked at him, her eyes filled with uncertainty. "Maybe."

"Do ya want me to look around?"

"You're probably right, but would you mind?"

Allison stuck by his side as he went from room to room downstairs. "Anything look wrong?" The place appeared pristine to him.

"Everything's fine."

He caught the nervous quiver still in her voice and gave her hand a reassuring squeeze as they continued their search on the second floor.

"I guess I just forgot to set it. I've never done that before."

They entered the last room upstairs. A decorative ceiling fixture bathed the raised bed in soft light. Like all the other rooms, this one looked untouched except for the slightly wrinkled comforter. In any other bedroom, he wouldn't have even noticed. However, after seeing how perfect everything else in the townhouse appeared, the minor wrinkles seemed out of place.

"This room is okay too."

Was there uncertainty in her voice? "Ya sure?" He couldn't explain it, but his gut told him something was off.

"It looks fine. Let's go back downstairs."

Rock eyed the entire room again, his eyes drawn to the large bed. For a heartbeat, he pictured Allison stretched out on it wearing nothing but a smile.

"Do you like flavored coffee? Or I can make you some espresso instead?" she asked from behind him.

Switching off the light and the image in his head, he followed Allison downstairs. "Whatever you're having is fine."

Taking a seat at the table, he watched Allison glide around the kitchen. To say she walked just didn't do justice to her graceful movements.

"How long have you lived here?"

"Since February." She glanced over her shoulder at him as

she poked around in the refrigerator. "Do you like milk and sugar in your coffee?"

"Black's good." Unlike most New Englanders, he preferred his coffee black and the stronger the better.

"That's good, because I'm out of milk." She carried over two mugs of coffee. "If it's too strong, let me know and I'll make a new pot. I like it that way and sometimes go a little overboard."

"No such thing as too strong."

His statement earned him a smile that left him a bit speechless.

"Not according to my brother Derek. He insists on making his own when he visits me. Then he loads it up with milk and sugar. By the time he's done, it's more like he's drinking a cup of hot coffee flavored milk."

Lifting the mug to her lips, she blew on the liquid before she closed her eyes and took a sip, somehow making the simple act of drinking coffee erotic. Once again growing uncomfortable, Rock reached for his own coffee. "Do you like it down here?" If he kept a conversation going, his brain would have something other than her lips to concentrate on.

"It's a little different than Rhode Island and I miss my family and friends, but I like it." She leaned forward, folding her arms on the table and giving him an excellent view of her breasts. "What about you? How does Virginia compare to other places you've lived."

Until that moment, he hadn't noticed the tiny birthmark on her left breast. Now that he'd seen it, he couldn't look away. *Answer her question.*

"It's better than some places I've been." Grabbing his mug, he drained it in one long swallow, ignoring the way the liquid burned his mouth and throat. "I've got an early morning. I should go." His eyes darted back to the birthmark and then back up at her eyes. "Thank you for the coffee."

"Anytime. I'll walk you to the door."

If it gave him another chance to watch her move, he wouldn't complain and tell her not to bother.

When they reached the foyer, he expected her to open the door. Instead, she reached for the doorknob and then let it go.

"Would you like to go out again?"

Now that classified as a Grade-A stupid question, and one requiring some thought regardless of what his dick said. This wasn't some base bunny asking him out for a cold beer and some fun sex. This was a high-society woman who called POTUS Uncle Warren.

Not counting when she asked Rock to act as her stand-in boyfriend for the night, she had never asked a man on a date. She'd never needed to. Tonight, an urgency to know him better gripped her. It had started the moment he picked her up and had grown as the night went on. Now, with him about to leave, she needed to do something while she still had the opportunity. Once he walked out the door, she might not get another chance.

His face remained expressionless. Had she misread him tonight?

No. She might have imagined the glances she thought he sent in her direction, but she hadn't imagined the hard erection she felt when they'd danced. No, it had been quite real.

"Not to another event like tonight's, promise. Something more casual. There are some nice restaurants in town. There's also a comedy club not far from here that Jake and Charlie love." Allison moved into his personal space. "Or we can do something closer to you. We don't have to stay in this area. Anywhere is fine."

His expression changed and he nodded.

When she opened the door for him earlier, she'd thought him panty-melting hot, but now as he smiled at her, she realized how wrong she'd been. Wow. Maybe it was a good thing the man didn't smile too often.

"How's next Saturday?"

She'd kind of been hoping for something sooner, but she wouldn't complain. He'd agreed. "Whatever works best for you."

He smiled again. Oh, yeah. He was protecting the female population by not smiling on a regular basis.

"I've got your number. I'll call ya later in the week and we can work out the details."

Well, she'd already done a first tonight and asked him out. She might as well do another first and kiss him, because it didn't look like he planned on doing it. "Great," she said, leaning closer and pressing a kiss against his lips. Since everything else about the man appeared hard, she expected his lips to be too. Instead, they were warm and pliant against hers.

Rough, callused hands settled on her bare back and traveled lower, sending a tingle down her spine, and she rubbed her tongue against his lips. On cue, his mouth opened and she didn't hesitate. Right away, she slipped her tongue inside.

He tasted like coffee and cherries. She'd noticed him popping hard candies on the ride into DC, as well as the ride home. She guessed they were the source of the cherry flavor.

Rock's hands moved again, settling on her butt, and an ache started between her legs. She hadn't had sex since before Halloween when she'd still been with Charles, and until this moment, she hadn't been the least bit aroused once in all that time. Now, she was considering another first and asking him up to her bedroom. Never in her life had she had sex on a first date. She left that type of behavior to her brothers. Before she got intimate with a man, she liked to know more than just his name. Right now, anything else about Rock seemed irrelevant. She wanted him and it was evident he desired her. There was no missing the erection pressing against her.

Then, just like that, his hands settled on her waist and he put space between their bodies. Cool reason immediately washed over her and heat warmed her face. She'd just been considering sex with a man she barely knew. If her brother Trent ever found out, he'd never let her live it down. She'd given him a hard time for sleeping with women he barely knew before he married Addie too often.

"I gotta go. We'll talk this week."

A stray piece of hair fell into her eyes and she pushed it away, glad it gave her something to do with at least one hand. "Great."

He gave her one last smile—which again had her reconsidering her 'need to know a man before sleeping with him' philosophy—and left.

Allison locked the front door and then double-checked the door in the kitchen. "What a night." On her way back through the front foyer, she tried the front door again before setting the alarm and heading up to bed. Not that she expected to fall asleep anytime soon. Between the coffee and the kiss, she expected to remain awake for sometime. At least upstairs she could relax in bed and fantasize about the handsome Marine she'd be seeing again soon.

CHAPTER 4

ABOUT TIME HE LEFT. From the safety of his bedroom, he watched Allison's unknown date for the night come down the steps. The guy paused once and turned to look at Allison's front door before he climbed into a black pickup. He didn't know the SOB's name, but it was the same jerk who had changed her tire outside Siena. Even from this distance, the dude was hard to miss. Soon though he'd know who the guy was. When he and Allison left, he'd copied down the jerk's license plate. A quick call to his friend Roger in the morning and he'd have the guy's name and address. Once he had the information, he'd decide what his next step would be. If he turned out to be some distant cousin or longtime family friend, he'd leave the guy alone. Otherwise, he'd do what he had to.

He glanced back at the townhouse when the pickup turned left and disappeared from sight. One by one, the lights on the first floor went off, leaving the rooms in darkness. He pictured Allison climbing the front staircase and entering the master bedroom. Looking up, he zeroed in on her bedroom window. How many times had he sat and stared at the windows, wishing he was inside with her? Too many, but soon that would end. Soon, she'd be his.

Unable to stop it, a smile spread across his face. Yes, soon, he'd be spending all his free time inside with her.

Light spilled out of Allison's bedroom moments before she appeared at the window. He only got a quick glimpse of her before she pulled the curtains. He didn't need to see her with his eyes though. He'd committed everything about Allison Sherbrooke to memory. Right now, he imagined her unzipping the sexy gown she'd worn tonight, a gown she should have been wearing for him. His smile died as he thought of the Marine who'd been with her.

Next time, she'll wear it for me. Allison's silhouette passed behind the curtain and he let his mind go back to undressing her. With the zipper undone, she'd slide the dress down over her perfect breasts. She'd let it pool down around her ankles, revealing her legs. Legs he wanted wrapped around his waist as he made love to her.

He gritted his teeth. Damn he wanted her. Tonight, he'd have to settle for someone else. As soon as he knew she was in bed, he'd pay Kitty a visit. She was always up for a little fun.

The light upstairs switched off. Allison was safely alone in her bed for the night. Now, he could leave. Later, he'd check back.

CHAPTER 5

ROCK GLANCED at the large screen television on the far wall while he waited for his buddy Connor. At the moment, the basketball game between Sacramento and Washington was on. Basketball wasn't his favorite sport, never had been. From time to time, he'd watch a game if he had nothing else to do, but he'd always preferred hockey and football. Tonight, various basketball games were on all the screens inside the sports pub near his apartment.

"Got tickets to this weekend's home game against Boston. I can't use them. You interested?" Connor asked, taking a seat across the scratched table. Like everything else in Shooter's Pub, the table had seen better days. However, the joint's run-down appearance didn't keep the customers away. The popular sports pub had a steady stream of regular customers every day of the week, many of them military men and women from the nearby base.

"I'll pass. Give Landon a call. He's a huge Boston fan."

"Asked him already. He's busy with the paralegal he's been seeing."

Something told him another of his friends would soon be making a visit to the church. Landon hadn't spent much time with anyone other than Lisa for the last six months. When he did go out without her, he didn't stop talking about her.

"Are you sure you don't want 'em?"

"Got plans this weekend." Plans he needed to finalize soon. He never said when he'd call, but it was already Wednesday. If they were going to do something on Saturday, he needed to get his ass in gear.

"If you think of anyone else that'd like 'em, let me know." Connor smiled at the waitress when she appeared at their booth and placed his drink order.

"Do you want another, sweetie?" Candy, the waitress, asked. She was a pretty redhead, and they'd flirted with each other a few times when he came in, and in the past, he'd enjoyed watching her move around the pub. She had a great bod and knew it, but tonight he'd forgotten she was there.

"Yeah, and an order of buffalo wings, please," Rock answered as his stomach rumbled loud enough to be heard over the blaring televisions.

"Bring over an order of regular ones too, Candy."

She gave them both smiles and an eyeful of her cleavage as she bent low to collect the menus she'd left on the table when Rock first sat down. "Be right back."

Across the table, Connor gave a low whistle as he watched her walk away. "Love the legs on that one. I've got to get her number before I leave."

He'd had a similar thought on previous visits himself, just not tonight. "What happened to Belle?" The last time he talked to Connor, he was dating an accountant.

With Candy and her legs no longer in view, Connor looked at him. "She moved back to Mississippi last month. She missed her family. No big deal." He shrugged, and Rock got the impression his friend wasn't all that broken up about it. "You still seeing that airline attendant. Susan, Suzanne?"

"Shana. We went out twice." And he wouldn't be calling her again. Near the end of their last date, she started talking about wedding dates and having kids. He didn't need any more red flags than that.

"Here you go, sweeties." Candy returned with their drinks. "Your wings will be out in a few minutes."

Once again, Connor watched the waitress walk away.

"Did you ask me to meet you here so you could watch her all night?" Rock asked.

"No, but since I'm here, why deny myself?" He picked up his beer bottle and took a swig as his eyes followed Candy until she disappeared through the kitchen door. Then, he turned his attention back to Rock. "You've heard of Elite Force Security, right?"

He'd heard of the expensive private security firm who provided protection to anyone who could afford them, including wealthy politicians and businessmen. Not that long ago, he'd read an article about them while in the dentist waiting room. "Yeah."

"They're recruiting. I gave them your name and number. I thought after this next trip to the sandbox you might be ready to retire and rejoin civilian life."

"I don't do babysitting." Following someone around so they felt safe while they shopped didn't interest him. "Can't believe you do." Connor always struck him as the type to stay in the Corps for life. When he'd announced he'd taken a position with Elite Force Security, Rock thought it was some kind of practical joke.

"There's more to the firm than personal security," Connor said, his eyes once again looking away from Rock.

"Two orders of wings. Do you need anything else?" Candy placed two plates overflowing with wings and some appetizer dishes on the table.

"How about a phone number?" Connor asked.

Candy didn't hesitate. She pulled a pen and pad from the apron around her waist, wrote what Rock guessed was her phone number down, and handed the paper to his buddy.

Connor shoved the paper into his pocket. "I'll call you."

The guy liked to pick up women. "That took ya longer than usual," Rock said once Candy left again. "Few months ago, you would've had her number before she brought our beers. Playing babysitter is slowing you down."

Connor filled his plate with wings before he glanced up at him. "I hear some jealousy. If you wanted her number, you should've said something sooner."

He had a date with Allison Sherbrooke this weekend, the hottest woman he'd ever talked to. Why would he want Candy's number when he had that to look forward to? While the waitress looked good in her short shorts and low-cut T-shirt, judging by the way she flirted with the male costumers, she'd probably slept with half the men who came in there, which was something a woman like Allison Sherbrooke would never do. *Mannaggia*, he had to call her. Tonight, he'd do it when he got home. He told himself the same thing yesterday, and yet never got around to it. He didn't put things off or avoid them no matter how unpleasant or painful. This phone call though was kicking his ass.

"Have all the fun you want with Candy. I told you, I have plans this weekend."

With a shrug, Connor licked the buffalo sauce from his fingers. "You'll probably hear from someone this week or next," he said, going back to what they were discussing before their food arrived.

"You might be ready for saving some spoiled heiress from a photographer who is threatening her with an extra-long camera lens, but I'm not."

"I don't do spoiled heiresses," Connor said, and then stopped and smiled. "Well, I would *do* one, but the firm has never assigned me the job of babysitting one." He grabbed another wing and added it to his plate. "When they call, sit down and hear 'em out."

His buddy had him curious. He'd known Connor a long time, and when he'd left the Corps to work as a glorified bodyguard, it hadn't fit. The guy's insistence now that they did more than just protect people from the paparazzi had him once again thinking about his friend's recent career change. If nothing else, hearing what the security firm had to say would satisfy his curiosity.

"Will do."

ALLISON ENDED her video conference call with Jake and checked off another item on her to-do list. With Jake out for the next two weeks, she'd promised to handle any pressing issues that couldn't wait until he got back. So far she'd managed to cross off the first two on her list. Assuming tomorrow's meeting with Bernstein Construction went well, she'd be able to cross off a third. Jake insisted she'd do fine, but after the rumors she'd heard about Dick Bernstein, she wasn't as confident. According to the gossip, Dick Bernstein was old school. He'd started the business with his father in the early 1950s and believed women belonged in the home taking care of the children, not the board-room. Somehow, she'd managed to avoid dealing with men like Bernstein up until now. Growing up, her father had always insisted she could do anything her brothers could. Her uncles shared a similar view. Even when she worked for her Aunt Marilyn at the Helping Hands Foundation, she managed to avoid chauvinistic men. If the rumors were true, tomorrow her streak would come to a halt.

Pulling the keyboard closer, Allison logged into her email. She checked it first thing this morning, but hadn't gotten around to it since. Now, her inbox contained two dozen new messages. She'd developed the habit of never leaving work without first emptying her inbox. Nothing was worse than starting a new workday with matters left over from the previous one. With some luck, whatever emails she'd received since this morning wouldn't require too much work. She'd like to leave on time tonight, or at least earlier than she had last night.

The first one she opened turned out to be nothing more than a message from Tasha Marshall inviting her up to a house party in the Hamptons. The Marshalls threw parties on a regular basis. From time to time, she'd attend one, but tonight she didn't even check to see if it fit her schedule before she typed a reply thanking Tasha for the invite and letting her know she couldn't make it.

She moved down the list, glad to see so far nothing in her inbox required much more than a yes or no reply. A knock at the door stopped her from opening the last one.

"Come in."

"Miss Sherbrooke, Mr. Bernstein's office called while you were on your video call. They need to reschedule tomorrow's meeting," Denise, the receptionist, said while walking into the office. "They said later in the month would work better for them."

"Thanks, Denise. I'll have Cindy reschedule the meeting in the morning when she comes in," she said, referring to Jake's executive assistant. If they wanted to postpone the meeting until the end of the month, Jake could handle it himself, and no one knew his schedule better than Cindy.

"And this came for you." Denise placed a brown teddy bear holding a box of her favorite chocolates down on her desk. "Unless you need something, I'm going to leave now."

"All set. I'm leaving soon too. Have a nice evening."

Allison waited until the receptionist left before she opened the card attached to the bear's ear. **Thought you'd like something sweet while you worked,** the typed message on the small notecard read. She could always use something sweet from Favre, a chocolate company she'd fallen in love with during a trip to Switzerland. Although well known in Europe, the company had only recently begun exporting to the United States.

Derek. The present had to be a joke sent from her twin brother. He loved to play jokes and harmless pranks on her. And it wouldn't be the first time he'd sent her a present and not signed his name to it. He'd done it once back in high school, only then he'd included "from your secret admirer" to the present. He knew where she worked and how much she loved Favre chocolate. Not many people knew either of those things. The present had to be from him. It was the only thing that made sense.

Allison flipped the card over to see if any other information was printed on the back. Perhaps if she called whoever delivered the bear, they'd tell her who ordered it. Except for flowers printed on the back of the card, it remained blank. "They're from Derek." Even as she repeated the words, a chill passed through her and she dropped the card. Later, she'd call him and confirm he'd sent the present. He may deny it at first, but if she hounded him enough, like a good twin sister, he'd eventually tell her the truth.

Pushing the bear and the chocolates into the far corner of her desk, she answered her final email and closed the Internet browser. Although she kept telling herself Derek sent the present, she didn't grab it when she gathered up her things and left for the night.

Traffic remained heavy through much of the city, and when she pulled into her driveway, she couldn't wait to get inside, slip on some PJs, and call Derek to get some answers. Once she satisfied her curiosity, she'd try her sister-in-law, Addie. Rock should be calling any day now to finalize their plans for the weekend, and when he did, she wanted it all mapped out. Since she didn't know him well, she hoped his sister would provide her with some ideas for their date.

Her entire townhouse remained in darkness until she used her keychain remote and switched on the lamp inside. Once the front hall was ablaze with light, she opened her car door. Inside, she punched in her alarm code, turning the system off, and then made sure she locked the front door behind her. She still didn't understand how she'd forgotten to turn the alarm on the night Rock picked her up. Despite the little voice that kept telling her she hadn't forgotten then either, logically she knew there was no other explanation.

"Come on, answer the phone," Allison said as she waited for her brother to pick up. She'd changed, popped a mini pizza in the oven, and decided to call Derek while she waited for the timer to go off.

Derek's recording came on after a few rings "Sorry I missed your call. Leave a message.".

Figures. "Thanks for the chocolates. Call me when you get this." He was good about returning her calls. Assuming it wasn't too late when he checked his messages, he'd call her back tonight.

With one call down and dinner not ready, she pulled up her sister-in-law's number and hoped she answered.

Like her first call, it rang a couple of times, but then Addie answered. "Allison, hang on a second.".

"Sure," Allison said, although she wasn't sure if Addie actually heard her or not. In the background, she heard noise as if her sister-in-law moved around. Then she came back on the line.

"Sorry. I wanted to finish putting the groceries away before Trent gets home. He thinks I shouldn't lift anything heavier than a pencil these days."

Allison heard the annoyance in Addie's voice and smiled. "I'd take advantage of that while you can."

"Trust me, you wouldn't. He's driving me crazy. At first, it was kind of sweet, but now, oh man."

"Not too much longer." She had a feeling Trent would be fretting over his wife even after she had the baby, but she kept her suspicions to herself. "If you're not busy, I need some help with something."

"Sure, I'm just waiting for Trent. We're going out with Gray and Kiera tonight."

Sometime soon, she needed to get up to Providence and visit her brother Gray and his fiancée. She'd spent some time with them earlier in the year when they'd first started dating, but had not seen them since they announced their engagement.

"What type of things does your brother like? We're supposed to go out Saturday night."

"He's letting *you* plan the date?" Addie's disbelief filtered over the phone.

"I asked him, so it seems like I should plan the night. Do you think he'll mind?"

"Probably not, and I'm glad you asked him. Give me a second to think."

The oven timer buzzed, and Allison pulled out her dinner while she waited for some suggestions and tried to come up with a few ideas of her own.

"He likes football, but the season is over."

Sports, she should have thought of that. "What about baseball?" She understood enough about baseball and could sit through a game.

"The season doesn't start until the beginning of April. You'd have to check the exact date."

Well, assuming their date this weekend went well, maybe a baseball game was something they could do next month together.

"He likes hockey. The regular season ends sometime in April, so there might be some games Saturday."

She didn't know the first thing about hockey other than the fact it was played on ice, but she'd give it a try. If there was a team in the area, she'd check and see if they had a home game this weekend. "I'll look into it. Anything else? Does he like the theater?"

"The only play I think he likes is *A Christmas Carol*. Again, wrong time of year. But maybe I'm wrong."

Planning this date was turning out to be more difficult than she anticipated. "What about music?" Numerous venues in the area featured live bands on the weekends.

"He likes the big hair bands from the 80s or anything that sounds like that, and classic hard rock similar to Trent."

Finding bands that fit Addie's description playing on Saturday would be a breeze. "I'll check for any hockey games first, and if there aren't any, I'll look for concerts. How about restaurants? Does he have a favorite type of food? Anything he absolutely hates?"

While her sister-in-law listed Rock's favorite types of food, Allison did a search for professional hockey teams on her tablet. She vaguely remembered a team called either Virginia or DC home, but she had no idea of their name. The list of professional hockey teams was much shorter than she expected. Scrolling through the names, she found the link for the team based out of DC and clicked on it. Immediately, the team's website popped up providing her with their entire schedule.

Perfect. They had a home game on Saturday. "Looks like we're heading to a hockey game," Allison said when Addie finished her sentence.

"Rock will love that. Can I help with anything else?"

"All set for now. Thanks for your help."

"Okay. Trent's home now, so we'll be going soon, but call later if you need me," Addie said. "If you don't mind, call me on Sunday. I'd like to hear how the night went."

After promising she would, Allison ended the call and turned her attention to eating dinner and planning out her and Rock's date. The game started at seven o'clock according to the website. That should give them enough time to grab a quick dinner before the game if they ate at a nearby restaurant. Or should they eat after the game so they didn't need to rush? How long was a hockey game anyway? With a search engine already open on her tablet, she typed the question in and right away a list of sites providing the answer came up.

The average hockey game lasted two-and-half hours. If they stopped for dinner after the game, it'd be closer to nine or nine thirty before they ate. She'd prefer to eat earlier than that. When

Rock called, she'd ask if he could pick her up around five so they could stop somewhere before the game. If he couldn't, she'd plan for dinner after the game and make sure she had a snack before he picked her up.

Speaking of snacks, she wished Derek would call her back soon. More than anything, she wanted to be right about the bear and chocolates being from him. Deep down, she couldn't accept it. Only once had he sent her something without his name on it, and it had been so long ago. Why would he do it now?

As if merely thinking of him conjured him up, Derek's ringtone erupted from her phone. She loved talking to Derek, but couldn't remember the last time she'd been so happy he called her back.

"How's my little sister?" Derek asked once she answered the phone. Although only five minutes older than her, he loved reminding her he'd been born first.

"You might be the older twin, but don't forget I'm the smarter one." It had always irked Derek that she'd scored eight points higher on her SATs than him and had graduated college with a higher GPA.

"Anyway, what's up? I got your message. Did you say something about chocolates?"

Another chill spread through her body, making tiny goose bumps appear on her arms. So he was denying he sent them. She'd expected that. "Knock it off, Derek. I know you sent the teddy bear and chocolates from Favre to the office today."

"I don't know what you're talking about. I didn't send anything. Didn't it come with a card?"

The chill seeped deeper inside her, sinking into her bones. "The card wasn't signed. It only said 'Thought you'd like something sweet while you worked' but I know you sent it. You know how much I love chocolate from Favre."

"Allison, honest, I didn't send you anything." The carefree tone he'd used when she answered the phone disappeared. "If you got something at work today, it was from someone else. Call the delivery company. Maybe they'll tell you who ordered it?"

Her scalp prickled as his words sank in. "I don't know where it came from. There was no business information on the card, just the typed message."

"Did whoever delivered it have on a uniform or a nametag?"

She should have thought of that. "I'll check with the receptionist tomorrow. It was left with her."

"Call the police."

"And tell them what? Someone sent me a present? There's not a law against sending gifts." Perhaps there should be though. "And don't tell anyone about this, especially Dad," she said before her brother could offer any other advice. If he opened his big mouth and told their dad, he'd probably hire a bodyguard to sleep outside her bedroom door, and then he'd be on the first plane to Virginia. He hadn't wanted her to move away from Providence in the first place. She loved her dad, but she didn't need him going into overprotective father mode. "You know how he gets sometimes."

"Getting gifts from strangers isn't normal, sis. I won't tell him if you promise to call the police or consider hiring some security for a little while."

She didn't want to do either, but she didn't need Derek calling their dad. "If it happens again, I'll call the personal security firm we've used in the past."

"No good. Either do it now or I'll do it for you, and then I'll let Dad in on what's happening."

Well, she could tell Derek what he needed to hear now and then do what she darn well pleased later. "Fine. I'll call the police in the morning." Derek was more likely to accept that answer from her than any other. He shared her sentiments when it came to having personal security around. "Happy?"

"I'd prefer if you called a security firm too. The police can't watch you twenty-four seven, but I know what a pain in the ass a bodyguard can be. Don't know how Uncle Warren stands having a shadow all the time. Promise me, if you get anything else, you'll get some personal security."

She didn't want to think about getting any other gifts. "I will. Cross my heart."

Derek's sigh came through the phone. "I don't like it, but okay. Give the police a call right now and if you need me, call. I can be there in a few hours."

Allison promised Derek again she'd call the police once they finished their conversation and then hung up. Most of the pizza she'd made remained on her plate, but her appetite was gone. Finding out a stranger was sending you gifts had a way of doing that.

So if Derek hadn't sent the teddy bear and candy, who did? It wouldn't be impossible to figure out where she worked. Her name and picture had been added to the Falmouth Foundation website, so a quick search of her name would bring up that information. But how would they know to send Favre chocolates? It certainly wasn't a chocolate every store stocked. In fact, few people in the States had even heard of it yet. Had the sender made a lucky guess, or was it someone she came in contact with on a regular basis? Or did she have a stalker out there? Someone who followed her around and watched where she went and what she bought.

She tried to push the last thought out of her mind. Unfortunately, the idea of a stalker brought back the memory of how her house security system hadn't been on Sunday night when she and Rock returned.

"I'm overreacting." She checked the lock on the kitchen door before tossing the cold pizza in the trash and heading out of the room.

She'd switched on the television and the lights in every room, yet she remained restless as she read articles about hockey on the Internet. If she and Rock were going to a game Saturday, she wanted to at least understand some of the basics. Unfortunately, her focus kept straying away from the information, and every time she heard even the tiniest of sounds, she jumped half a mile out of her chair.

Since she'd moved to Virginia, she'd been a little on edge. More than once she'd been out and gotten the feeling someone watched her. Each time it happened, she told herself it was her imagination. She'd almost completely convinced herself of that until her car accident. She hadn't been far from Jake's house when she spotted the headlights behind her. At first she'd thought it was just someone heading in a similar direction. Then they'd gotten much closer and stayed right on her bumper for a good ten minutes. Unsure if the car was following her or not, she turned so she could return to her cousin's. Like a shadow, the car had done the same. Shaken up, she started checking her rearview mirror more and more the closer she got to Jake's neighborhood. Caught up in what was going on behind her, she hadn't seen the other car skid on the slick roads and plow though the intersection and into her car. If she'd been paying attention, she might have been able to stop or swerve out of the way. Thankfully, the worst of her injuries had been a broken leg, and the driver of the other car had only needed some stitches.

She hadn't told anyone about the car behind her that night. Instead, she'd convinced herself it had been a coincidence. The little bear and candy at the office had her reconsidering her belief. From now on, she'd need to be extra vigilant while out alone.

Unable to focus on anything, she gave up reading about hockey and the responsibilities of each player. The game wasn't until Saturday. She had Thursday and Friday night to learn more about the rules. Picking up the remote, she flipped through the stations until she found the popular new sitcom she'd started watching in the fall. The show didn't require much brainpower and always made her laugh. It was the kind of show she needed tonight.

∾

THE SPECIFICS of their date still eluded him. How could he plan an evening out when they had zilch in common? Regardless, he'd promised he'd call, and he never backed out of a promise. Rock dropped his wallet and keys on the counter and brought up Allison's number on his smartphone. He'd stored it in his contact list the night he'd joined her, Trent, and Addie for dinner but hadn't thought he'd need it. The phone rang several times, and he expected her voicemail to pick up soon. When it did, he'd leave her a message, and if she was still interested in going out, she could call him back. If she'd changed her mind, he would have fulfilled his promise.

Her voicemail never picked up. Instead, her sultry voice greeted him. "Hello."

"Allison, it's Rock."

"Rock, hi." The hint of uncertainty he'd detected in her voice when she first answered disappeared. "I'm glad you called. I've been planning our night out."

Having a woman plan an evening out was a first for him. He only hoped whatever she had in mind didn't include the ballet or some equally ridiculous event. Once he'd been forced to attend the ballet as part of a school fieldtrip. He'd fallen asleep a quarter of the way through and stayed that way until his teacher rudely woke him up with a boney finger to the shoulder.

He had no desire to see guys running around in tights again, and nothing except perhaps a 9mm pistol pressed up against his back would get him back to the ballet.

"I already ordered tickets for the hockey game. It starts at seven. There's a great barbecue restaurant not far from here. I thought we could have dinner there before we head into DC. Or we can stop somewhere after the game. Up to you. Either works for me."

The words hockey and Allison Sherbrooke didn't belong in the same sentence. She struck him as the refined, theater-going, opera-loving socialite portrayed in the movies. No movie he'd ever watched showed a woman like Allison drinking beer and cheering at a hockey game. "Sounds good." If she'd ordered them already, he'd keep his mouth shut and be damn happy she hadn't bought tickets to the ballet instead. "When do you want me to pick ya up?"

"How does around five sound?"

"That works."

"Great. I'll see you Saturday night," Allison said, sounding as eager as he felt.

"See ya." Rock hung up and ran a hand down his neck. The woman kept throwing him. He'd pegged Allison as your typical socialite, similar to those in the media, the kind of woman who liked lots of attention and only the best of everything. Her actions blew that theory out of the water. In fact, if he hadn't known who lurked on her family tree, he would've assumed she was just any other woman. A woman who'd planned what he'd consider a perfect night out.

He could accept that she liked barbecue. Lots of people did. But hockey? He didn't buy that one. They talked about a lot of things the night he escorted her to the fundraiser, but not sports. While hockey had its loyal fans, it wasn't as popular as football or baseball. The only way she would've known he enjoyed the game was if she'd asked his sister. Would she have bothered calling Addie? A few months ago, he would've said hell no. Why would she go out of her way, when men probably bent over backward for her all the time? Tonight, however, it was the only explanation, which meant his sister was going to love telling him she'd been right.

Hell.

CHAPTER 6

ROCK MULLED over his earlier convo with Eric Coleman as he vacuumed his truck, not that it needed to be done. Much like his apartment, he kept his truck spotless and he'd vacuumed it right before the fundraiser. Still, it gave him something to do. He'd spent as much time as he could at the range earlier, shooting both his 9mm pistol as well as the .44 magnum revolver he'd purchased last month. Only the fact that he'd run out of practice ammo had sent him packing.

Thanks to Connor, he'd been expecting a call from Elite Force Security ever since he met him for a beer. When Thursday and Friday passed but no call came, he assumed the security firm had rejected Connor's recommendation. He was good with that. Then Coleman called this morning.

He hadn't given Rock a ton of specifics over the phone, but he'd read between the lines. The firm definitely did more than provide bodyguards. Exactly what else they did still remained a secret. Intrigued by the little bit of information Coleman gave him, he agreed to a face-to-face meeting in a few weeks. Well, the firm's director called it a meeting. Rock got the impression it was more of an interview and most likely a waste of his time. He loved what he did and saw no reason to make any changes at the present. Elite Force would have to offer him something irresistible to get him to leave the Marines. No matter how much he thought about it, he couldn't think of anything Coleman could say or offer that fit the bill, except perhaps Allison Sherbrooke naked and in his bed.

Mannaggia, she was the living, breathing definition of irresistible. But it was safe to say the director wouldn't be offering her up as an incentive to change careers.

The single thought of her brought back the memory of his hands on her ass while they'd danced. Damn, the thing had been perfect. He hadn't fully recovered from the experience when she planted a kiss on him. Thanks to her, he suffered with a boner the entire ride home. Only an ice-cold shower before bed had helped enough for him to fall asleep.

He hoped he got a chance to touch her ass again and maybe find out if it was as smooth as the skin on her back and arms. The woman must bath in baby oil or something. He'd never felt skin so smooth. Without a doubt, he could've stood in her townhouse all night and just ran his hands up and down her back.

Get your head on straight. He stood a better chance of getting hit in the head with a puck at the hockey game than he did of getting his hands on Allison's ass or anywhere else tonight. He'd met and dated enough women to know she wasn't the type to sleep with a guy she barely knew.

Turning off the car vacuum, Rock hung the hose back up on the wall. He had another hour to kill before he headed toward Alexandria. It wouldn't take him long to shower and dress, but he didn't really have enough time to do anything else right now either. He might as well go home.

One of his favorite 80s rock songs came on, and he cranked up the volume as he tried a new route back. He'd lived in the area for eleven months now, and until last week, the bridge near the carwash had been closed for construction. The guy in the apartment next door claimed it was a better route with fewer traffic lights. Now seemed as good a time as any to give it a try.

He turned the music up another notch as one of his all-time favorite guitar solos started, the very one that had sent him begging his parents to let him take guitar lessons. It had taken him a solid month to convince them, but eventually they gave in. He hadn't stopped playing since, although he still couldn't do this solo justice.

In the parking lot behind his building, he killed the engine and heard his phone beep.

Call me before you go out tonight, the message read.

It was from Addie; that confirmed his suspicion. Allison had called her before planning out their evening. He still had time on his hands. A convo with his little sister, although she wasn't looking too little these days, would shave some more minutes off the clock. Crossing the lot, he pulled up his sister number. She answered before he opened his building's front door.

"I didn't think you'd call me back," she said in lieu of a greeting.

"Don't say it."

"Say what? I was right."

He glanced toward the ceiling as he unlocked his apartment door. His sister could be insufferable sometimes. "There's a first for everything." He loved pushing his sister's buttons, probably more than she enjoyed doing it to him. "Enjoy it while you can."

"After that insult, I need to reconsider asking you to be the baby's godfather."

Her comment left him without a good comeback. Addie got along well with all of them; however, she'd always been closer to him than their older brothers. Despite that, he'd assumed when the time came, Addie and her husband would pick one of Trent's brothers to be the baby's godfather. If anyone could provide for their son or daughter, it was one of them.

"It's a good thing I didn't want to talk about it tonight," she said in her 'I'm pretending to be mad' voice. "What are you guys doing tonight? Game? Concert?"

"Dinner and a hockey game. She called you, didn't she?"

"Allison wanted to know some things you enjoyed. I gave her a few suggestions. And now I have one for you. She loves flowers. Bring her some tonight."

He didn't even know where the closest florist was located. "I've been out with women before. I don't need dating advice."

"I'm only trying to help. I really like Allison and want you guys to have a nice night. I think she'd enjoy getting some roses or something from you."

Grabbing some flowers wouldn't kill him. "If I see a florist, I'll think about stopping." Allison had made an effort planning the evening. Maybe he should too. "Anything else you think I should know?"

"Avoid belching at the table. Oh, and don't use your pants as a napkin either."

"Shove it, Addie." He didn't need her wise-ass comments tonight.

"You're uptight. I'm only joking with you." She paused, and he heard her take in a deep breath. "This baby is going to be a soccer player. Either that or a kicker on a football team. He never stops."

Rock didn't miss the pronoun in her sentence. "You're having a boy? Didn't ya just tell us at dinner you and Trent don't know."

"We don't. Honest. Something keeps telling me we're having a boy though. It's weird. Either way, I'm looking forward to not being sick every morning," she answered. "Anyway, have fun and enjoy yourself tonight."

He had a smart, beautiful woman to himself for the next several hours. He definitely planned on enjoying every minute of it.

ROCK ENTERED Arrangements by Gertrude and stopped. Flowers

of every color, shape, and size filled the florist shop two blocks away from Allison's townhouse. Where the hell should he start?

"Can I help you?" a grandmotherly sort wearing a pink apron, who didn't even reach his chest, approached him.

"I need a bouquet of flowers, ma'am." Since he stood in a joint surrounded by flowers, his need should be obvious to the employee.

"Please call me Gertie." She pointed to her nametag and smiled. "What did you have in mind?"

Beats me. "I'm not sure."

"Well, are they for a special occasion?"

Did it really matter? "A night out. Can you put together something you'd like to get?" Gertrude might be old enough to be his Nonna, but she was the only woman around to help him at the moment. Hopefully, if she made something she liked, Allison would too.

Gertrude rubbed her hands together and gave him a smile that made him suspect this little gift was going to cost him a pretty penny. "Certainly, does your lady have a favorite flower I should include?"

He should've asked his sister about Allison's favorites. "She likes just about everything." No way was he telling Gertrude here he didn't know what Allison liked. "Don't put in any roses," he added before she got to work. Every well-dressed suit Allison went out with probably brought her roses. He wanted something that would stand out.

"Give me a few minutes and I'll put together something perfect," the florist said, eyeing the refrigerated cases of flowers as if she was about to lay siege to them.

A woman with a mission. He watched Gertrude go from one case to another, plucking out colorful flowers and adding them to the growing bouquet in her hand. Occasionally, she'd put something back and then pick out something else.

A few minutes turned into ten, but when she handed him the

final product, even he recognized what a beautiful arrangement she'd put together for him.

"Your lady friend is going to love this," she said, handing him the bundle she'd wrapped in clear plastic before tying a dark purple ribbon around it.

He hoped so. "Thank you for your help, ma'am."

"Enjoy your night out," she called as he walked toward the door, "and stop back in anytime."

He intended to enjoy it, but he didn't see himself stopping in again.

Rock bit down on the cherry flavored candy in his mouth and circled around the block. On his first pass, there hadn't been any open spots in front of Allison's townhouse. If he didn't see any now, he'd park on the next street over and hoof it. Turning the corner, he noticed the silver sedan flying up behind him. At the last moment, it slowed down, but it continued to ride his bumper all the way down Washington Street. Driving so close during rush hour traffic, he got, but not now. If the guy wanted to be a jerk, he could be too. Rock slowed his speed, forcing the other driver to either slow down too or plow into the bed of his truck.

What's it going to be, jerk? Thanks to the other car's dark-tinted windows, he couldn't see the driver's face, but Rock doubted the dude was happy as he backed off. As he turned onto Cameron Street again, the silver sedan did the same while still maintaining a decent distance.

Had everyone in Alexandria decided to park on this street tonight? Cars still lined Allison's side of the road. He'd have to park on Washington and walk. Once again, he turned a corner and checked his rearview mirror. Whoever had been behind him turned in the opposite direction.

He pulled into the first open spot he saw.

He eyed the bouquet as he opened his truck door. Not bad, but not worth the money he'd dished out for something that would be dead and wilted in a few days. Women, he'd never understand them.

A steady stream of traffic zipped up and down the street, forcing him to wait. At the first break in the traffic, he stepped off the curb and paused, his gut telling him someone or something was out of place. Crossing the street, he assessed his surroundings. Several people walked on the sidewalks, but none sent up any red flags. He checked each of the parked cars. As far as he could tell, they were all empty.

He'd learned to listen to his instincts. They'd saved him more than once. So what was he missing? He glanced at the parked cars again as he approached Allison's door. *Nothing.* "*Merda*," he muttered, another of his favorite Italian curses, as he climbed Allison's steps. Until he identified the who or what, he couldn't do anything about it. In the meantime, he'd keep an eye out.

Ringing the doorbell, he waited and assessed his surroundings. Or he did, until the door opened.

How he'd gotten so lucky, he didn't know and didn't care. Damn, how could a woman dressed so casually manage to look hot and sophisticated at the same time?

"Come on in." Smiling, she stepped back.

How long would it take to kiss off her lipstick? Would she even let him? Now might not be the time to find out, so instead, he held out the flowers. "These are for you." *Brilliant thing to say, Raimono. Of course she knows they're for her. You just walked into her house carrying the stupid things.*

Accepting the bouquet, she closed the door and approached him. "They're gorgeous. Thank you. Let me put them in water and grab my jacket." Rather than walk past him, she rested her palm on his shoulder, her fingers brushing against his neck as she kissed his cheek, sending his blood into a low simmer. "I hope you're hungry. Cooper's Smokehouse has the best barbecue."

Not even a monk would've been able to resist kissing Allison with her standing so close. And he was no monk. "Starving." *But not for food.* Dipping his head, he took her lips.

Beneath his, Allison opened her mouth and traced his lips, sending out an unspoken message. One he heard loud and clear. Opening his mouth, he waited for her to make the next move. Right away, she dipped her tongue inside, teasing his and causing his pulse to march double time.

She knows how to kiss. His hands itched to move lower than her waist. Instead, he pulled her closer, pressing her body into his and taking control of their kiss.

He could've happily stayed just where he was all night, but crinkling plastic reached his ears and Allison pulled away. "Come on. I keep the vases in the kitchen." She tugged on his hand, leaving him no other choice but to follow her. Not that he minded. At the moment, he'd follow her into a raging firefight.

With care, she snipped each stem before placing it in the glass vase, telling him she had a lot of practice at the task. If he'd wanted to make an impression, he should have brought her something other than flowers. *Too late now.*

She had almost all the stems cut when she stopped. "Did you send something to my office this week?"

The unease in her voice more than her question reinforced his instincts from earlier that something wasn't right. "No." So what if she got a gift at work? It was none of his business. He saw her hand shake when she added the last flower to the vase. "What did ya get?" He only asked because she appeared upset, not because he cared if other men sent her things.

"Some candy. It's no big deal. I'd just like to know who sent it." She shrugged and stuck the last flower into the vase. "All set to go."

She better never play poker, because Allison couldn't lie, but if she wanted to pretend the gift didn't bother her, he'd play along tonight.

∼

ASKING if he'd sent the candy and bear had been stupid. Even before she spoke, she knew the answer. A guy like Rock didn't send furry teddy bears with notes that said **Thought you'd like something sweet while you worked**. Then again, he didn't seem like the flower-giving type either, but she had a beautiful bouquet in her kitchen.

When she'd opened her door and saw them in his hand, she'd done a double take. Dates showed up with similar arrangements all the time. While she appreciated the gesture, it didn't warm her from the inside out. Seeing Rock standing there holding them had done just that. How could seeing a big, tough guy like him holding something so delicate do anything else? Even now, while they waited for their waitress to return with their drinks, the memory made her smile. Then there had been his kiss. Holy moly, what a kiss. She'd only ended it because the alternative would've been hitting the sheets rather than watching hockey players hitting the boards. Hitting the boards, she thought that was the correct phrase anyway.

Inhaling, she savored the smell of sweet barbecue filling one of her favorite restaurants in Alexandria. Other than her twin brother, no one knew she loved chicken or ribs covered in barbecue sauce. She didn't really care which style sauce. As long as it was authentic, not the gross bottled stuff sold in stores, and she had plenty of napkins while eating it, she was happy. She couldn't imagine any of the men she'd dated in the past sharing her enjoyment of the somewhat messy cuisine. Rock seemed like the type who would, which was why she picked Cooper's tonight.

"Everything here is great, but I recommend the chicken with Kentucky Black Barbecue Sauce. If you get pork, get the South Carolina Mustard Sauce." Allison read the specials listed on the paper stuck inside the menu, each one sounding better than the one before it.

"You've been here before?"

Talk about a silly question. She'd suggested this place,

hadn't she? Who would suggest a restaurant they'd never eaten at? "Yep, and that surprises you because…?"

He put his menu down, and she watched the way his shirt stretched over his shoulders and biceps. His long shirtsleeves did nothing to hide his well-defined arms. And while she had a fabulous imagination, one of these days, she'd like to see just what his shirt hid from view.

"I thought you'd prefer places like Siena. Barbecue can be messy."

He didn't know her well yet, so she understood his assumption, even if she didn't like what it implied.

"When you suggested this, I thought maybe it was my sister's idea too."

At least he's honest. Too many times in the past, she'd gone out with men who said what they thought she wanted to hear. "Nope. I get takeout from here a lot. My cooking skills are limited. But I did get the idea of a hockey game from her." He'd know soon enough she knew next to nothing about hockey, despite her recent efforts.

Rock gave her another one his steam-producing smiles, and Allison hoped no other women in the restaurant noticed. If they had, she might have trouble getting him out of there later. "Guessed as much. She told me you liked flowers, and Gertie the florist picked them out."

"Gertie is a sweetie. I stop in there about once a week and pick something up. I like fresh flowers in my office and house."

"She reminded me of my Nonna."

"That's Italian for grandmother, right? Do you speak it? I learned Spanish and German in high school, but they didn't have Italian."

"I'm not fluent, but I know enough keywords to get by." He reached out for his water glass, his movements once again pulling her eyes with him. "You don't know anything about hockey, do ya? We can skip the game if you want. Go somewhere else."

"Nope, but I've been reading up about hockey this week and the tickets are in my purse."

He cocked an eyebrow and nodded. "Let's see what you've learned," he said good-naturedly. "How many players does each team have on the ice at one time?"

At least he's starting with the easy questions. Sure, she'd read a few articles, but she didn't think all that much had sunk in. That tended to happen when she wasn't all that interested in a subject. "Six."

"And what are their positions?"

"Goalie, center..." She hesitated, trying to remember the rest. *Think.* She'd just read about the players and their positions last night. "Right and left something." She cringed. Wow, she sounded real intelligent.

"Left and right wings," he said with a smile.

Right, those position names had made her think of birds. "And two defensemen." She gave herself a mental pat on the back and hoped he didn't ask her to go into each player's responsibilities.

"You got it. Do ya remember what each one does?"

Oh well, so much for that wish. "The goalie tries to keep the puck out of the net. The right wing is responsible for the right side of the ice." She had the goalie part right; as far as the rest, she was grasping at straws.

"That's part of it. If ya want, I can give you a quick crash course."

If it meant she could listen to his voice, her answer was a resounding yes. "I'm all ears. Go for it."

Like an encyclopedia of all things hockey, Rock launched into an easy-to-understand explanation of what each player did before he started on the general rules of the game. From time to time, she interrupted with a question, but truthfully she enjoyed listening to his voice too much to stop him. Only when dinner arrived did their conversation slow down as they ate.

Her friends didn't know what they were missing by not

eating barbecue. Resisting the urge to lick some sauce from her thumb, she grabbed a napkin. Across from her, Rock finished off the rib in his hand and reached for another one. Much like the rest of him, his hands were large and tanned, making her wonder if he spent a lot of time outside. Right now, she wouldn't mind having a little of his color. Every winter, she turned into a pale ghost until the spring rolled around and she could spend time outdoors again. Thanks to the milder temps, she started spending more and more time outside this month, but her color had a long way to go. Judging by the color in his hands and face, it didn't look like the weather kept him stuck inside.

"Anything else I need to know before the game?" Allison pulled open a wet napkin so she could wipe her sticky fingers. If she ate another bite, she'd explode, and she'd only eaten about a quarter of her meal. Judging by the size of their portions, the restaurant thought they were serving giants.

"I gave ya the basics, and if ya don't understand something later, just ask."

"Fair enough." She glanced briefly at her ringing cell, which stuck out of her purse's front pocket. No phone number was displayed, only the words **No Caller ID.** Whoever was calling either had an unlisted number or knew someway to keep it from showing up. Since it wasn't a relative and she couldn't think of anyone who would need to talk to her now, she ignored the phone. Tomorrow, when she went through her lazy Sunday morning routine, she'd call whoever it was back.

Rock dropped the bone he'd cleaned off and reached for a wet napkin too. "Gonna answer that?" he asked, once again replacing a words proper ending with an 'a' instead.

"I'll call them back tomorrow." The music from her phone stopped. "If we're hungry after the game, I thought we could stop at Carolina's Bakery. Their tiramisu isn't as good as at your grandfather's bakery, but it's a close second."

"Customers love his recipe. Between you and me, I hate tiramisu."

"Not a very good Italian, are you?"

"Can't stand calamari either. When I was a kid and Nonna served it, I'd give it to my brother, Jon, when she wasn't looking so I could still get dessert. She had this thing about not getting anything else until you cleared your plate."

The image of him passing off his food when his grandmother turned her back made her smile. "I won't tell her. And everything else at Carolina's is delicious too."

"Whatever you want tonight, I'm up for it."

The smartphone she'd ignored moments ago started up again with the same message on the screen.

Rock plucked the phone from her purse and handed it to her. "Someone wants ya. Take it. I don't mind."

"It's probably some reporter trying to get information about Jake and Charlie's son. They've refused to give out any pictures or details about Garret, and the media doesn't like being left out." Without answering it, she turned off the phone and stuck it back into her purse. "I'm not ruining our night by talking to them. Let them leave a message." Grabbing his hand, she gave it a squeeze. "Come on, let's see how much I learned from you so far tonight."

ON A SCALE of one to ten, with a one being "I'd rather be sorting my sock drawer than out with this guy" and a ten being "Please don't let this night end," the evening ranked at a nine. If not for the permanent chill that had seeped into her body, she would've given the night a ten. And the chill was her fault. She'd bought tickets to an ice hockey game. Ice, the keyword in the sentence. She should've considered it would be chilly inside the arena when she'd picked her clothes for the night. Instead, she'd been more concerned with looking nice. Next time, she'd know better. And there would be a next time if she had anything to say about it.

She couldn't remember the last time she'd been on a date and just been herself. Not once during dinner or the ride into DC had she worried Rock was with her because of some personal ambitions. When he asked questions, she hadn't worried a wrong answer would somehow find its way into the media. Although he hadn't asked a ton of questions, the ones he had asked had been direct and personal without being intrusive. While she had nothing to hide, some information she'd rather not share on a first date. A lot of men she went out with didn't understand that. Perhaps they thought, since the media butted into her family's life so much, they could too. Men like that didn't get a second date. And already she was planning one with Rock, assuming he was open to the idea. She got the definite impression he would be.

On the ice, player number ten got possession of the puck and skated down the rink toward the net. Allison scooted to the edge of her seat, unable to look away. If the player made the goal, it would put the Capitals up and she wanted them to win. After all, they were the home team, since she now lived in the area.

She cringed when a player from the other team checked number ten, and then she almost laughed. She'd expected to hate hockey and find it as boring as soccer, a sport both her and Derek had tried as kids. While Derek had loved it and gone on to play for several years, she'd begged her parents to let her quit before the season hit the halfway point. Despite her pleas, they'd made her finish out the season, insisting she'd made a commitment to the team. After that experience, she'd avoided traditional team sports and stuck with dancing and tennis.

Oddly though, she didn't hate hockey or find it boring. Actually, if she'd known she was going to enjoy the game this much, she would've given it a try a long time ago. Of course some of her enjoyment might be due to her company for the evening.

Throughout the first half of the game, Rock continued his lessons. As soon as the players took the ice, he pointed out which player was in what position. If a penalty got called and wasn't obvious why, he explained it. Once or twice, she almost asked him questions just to hear his voice. With a voice like his, the man should be doing television commercials and narrating books or something.

Down on the ice, number thirteen went into the boards and dropped like a stone to the ice as the referee blew his whistle. Allison held her breath and watched, waiting for the player to move as whom she guessed was a team trainer and the coach came out to him.

"He's not moving, is he?" Suddenly, the game wasn't as much fun anymore.

"Doesn't look like it. Guys get knocked out sometimes." He said it as if they were discussing the weather rather than another human's wellbeing.

A stretcher appeared and the player was moved onto it. Before he could be rolled away though, the player gave the crowd a thumbs up, letting everyone know he was at least awake.

"I hope he's okay." Almost as soon as the stretcher left, a player came off the bench and took number thirteen's place.

"The guy probably has a concussion. Happens a lot in hockey and football."

Football was another game she didn't know much about, but she could see how concussions would be common. The game did involve grown men routinely banging heads. Even if they did wear helmets, that couldn't be good for you. In fact, her parents had forbid any of her brothers from playing football in school.

Less than a minute later, the buzzer sounded, signaling inter-mission, and "Rock You Like A Hurricane" filled the arena as people headed for food or the restrooms.

Unable to stop herself, she sang along with the chorus until she looked over and saw Rock staring, not just looking, at her. "What? My singing isn't that bad, is it?" She realized she'd never land a recording contract, but she hadn't thought her singing was terrible either, despite what Derek said.

"No. Just surprised *you* know this. Guessed you'd be more into whatever's hot on the radio."

They hadn't discussed music, so his assumption made sense. "Usually I am, but I like the Scorpions. I have ever since I danced to a version of this song in a recital one year."

"That's wrong."

Was he teasing her? She couldn't tell. "The recital had an 80s theme to it. All the dance numbers, even the ballet ones, were done to songs from the 1980s. I danced to four different 80s songs that year. I only liked this one though and bought some of their best hits CDs. I think I still have them somewhere." She wouldn't admit to anyone, but she hated to throw things out.

"There's a local tribute band that plays their music. I've seen them play a few times. They're not bad."

"I didn't know that. What's their name?"

"Trance."

"I'll look them up. If they have a show soon, let's go."

"Their concerts get rowdy sometimes," he warned.

Okay, she thought he was interested in getting to know her and spending time with her. Had she read him wrong? Had he agreed to this date to be nice? Allison dismissed her thoughts right away. If he'd only said yes to be nice, he sure as heck wouldn't have brought her flowers and kissed her the way he had. So how should she interpret his statement? "All concerts get a little crazy sometimes. It doesn't bother me." She'd attended tons of concerts as a teenager and in college. This band's couldn't be that much different.

"The last one I went to, three fights broke out inside and the cops arrested a few drunks in the parking lot."

That sounded a little rowdier than she was accustomed to, but nothing she couldn't handle, assuming she wasn't alone. "I'd be fine."

Down on the ice, the players took their positions, but Rock didn't seem to notice as he leaned closer. "You're serious."

It hadn't sounded like a question, but she couldn't stop herself from nodding anyway.

He smiled, and whatever chill she had before disappeared, replaced with enough heat to melt the entire rink.

"Okay." He moved closer still and kissed her lips, making her wish she hadn't pulled her jacket on.

Before she got the chance to really get into the kiss and enjoy it, he pulled away. Rather than turn his attention to the game, he scanned the crowd. "Someone's watching us."

The man with the camera pointed in their direction was difficult to miss, and she mentally kicked herself. She should've warned him that going on a date or anywhere else with her meant your picture might end up on the Internet or some magazine cover. Especially lately. In the past, the media had been content to shadow her cousins and brothers. Now though with Jake and Trent happily married and both Sara and Gray engaged, the media needed new blood. Hence they'd turned their sights and camera lenses on her.

"Sorry. I should've warned you that might happen." *Please don't let it bother you.* With the exception of one guy she'd dated a few times in college, the men she went out with were not bothered by the media attention that sometimes found her. A few even clamored for it. However, she could see it annoying Rock. She just didn't know if it would annoy him enough to say *adios* or not.

Rock's eyes darted in the direction of the photographer again before he met her gaze. "Dude didn't get much of a pic, did he? What do ya say we give him a better one?"

She swore his eyes twinkled as he spoke. "Let's."

CHAPTER 7

LOOKED like he needed to change his plans. Up until now, he'd held off, unsure if it was necessary or not. Instead, he'd watched and waited, dividing his time between here and Dumfries so he could keep an eye on Rocco Raimono, which turned out to be a surprisingly easy thing to do. The guy was predictable. Every morning that week, he'd gone for a run before the damn sun even came up. Two of the days, he ran with a friend, but the other four he went alone. Then, except for this morning, he drove to the Marine base in Quantico, where he spent the bulk of the day. He'd considered trying to get on base to learn more but decided it would only bring attention his way. Attention he didn't want. Besides, it didn't really matter what the SOB did on base. He only cared about what he did off. Once Raimono left the base, he returned home, where he stayed until the next morning. The only night he'd done anything differently had been Wednesday. He'd gone straight from the base to Shooter's Pub where he'd spent a couple of hours before leaving alone.

He'd been confidant Raimono didn't pose any threat and readied to leave Dumfries for good. Then tonight he saw the guy's pickup pull out of his apartment's parking lot, and something told him to follow the SOB one last time. Sure enough, he'd headed north toward Alexandria.

He'd gotten good at following and not being noticed. Something snapped though when he saw Raimono walk out of Arrangements by Gertrude with a huge bouquet. Rage had burned in his chest and he'd gotten sloppy. Raimono had noticed him behind him. Even after he'd backed off and parked, the guy had been vigilant, checking his surroundings, which was why he was sitting at home with no idea where his love was. Following the couple again once they left her townhouse had been too risky. Right now, Raimono didn't know for certain he'd been followed. If he spotted the same car behind him again tonight, however, it would raise his suspicions. He couldn't allow that to happen, especially when he was this close to having the woman he loved. No, until he figured out the best way to get Raimono out of the equation, he needed to back off a little.

CHAPTER 8

A WEEK AGO, he hadn't even known there was a Botanic Garden in DC, let alone cared to visit it. Yet, he was now heading down Maryland Avenue toward what the Internet described as a living plant museum. As if plants needed a museum of their own. But if he was bored to death for the next few hours, it was his own damn fault. Since Allison had planned their last outing with his preferences in mind, he'd wanted to return the favor. A flower-loving woman like Allison should love an afternoon gaping at flowers from around the world followed by a picnic lunch in Bartholdi Park. A picnic lunch he'd already ordered but they'd need to pick up once Allison either got bored of flower gazing or he passed out from hunger.

Judging by the way her face lit up when he announced their destination, he suspected the second would happen long before the first. And damn but her expression was still alive and well in his mind. Any suffering he experienced today looking at fucking plants was worth the smile she'd given him. That smile had made his heart jump, and he'd been unable to resist kissing her. Then again, no matter what her expression, he found it difficult not to kiss her. Any straight guy with eyes would suffer from the same problem.

"Do ya want a guide?" Rock asked when they entered the building and passed by a display containing visitor guides in every language imaginable.

She gave his hand a little squeeze. "I think I could write the guide myself I've been here so many times. Do you care where we start?"

"I'm following you."

"This way then. I love checking out the orchids. Every time I come, there are different ones in bloom."

Orchids, those were the big white flowers his mom bought Nonna every Easter, right? Did a museum need to dedicate a whole section to them? Wouldn't a shelf or two do?

"My mom tried growing orchids in her greenhouse, but she never had much success. She even traveled to the Philippines and handpicked the ones she wanted. They still didn't survive. Her roses and gardenias were breathtaking."

Trees and rocks filled the glass room she led him into. Flowers like he'd never seen before clung to the branches and sprouted from the vegetation growing close to the floor. Humid air filled the space, reminding him of the rainforest in South America—a place he didn't have particularly good memories of and no wish to spend time in again.

"Aren't they beautiful?" Allison released his hand as she bent to examine a light purple flower. "These are dendrobium orchids. Mom should've tried growing these. They tend to be easier than some of the others."

"When you said orchid, I pictured the white flowers the stores sell around Easter." He looked around the room but didn't see anything that resembled those.

"You're thinking of lilies. Those are pretty too, but I like these more."

To him, a flower was a flower.

"Let's see what else is out today. Usually there are a few hundred different orchids blooming at the same time in here."

That explained the unique smell. It was like someone had

taken a few bottles of perfume and mixed it with some damp soil before spreading it around the room. While not unpleasant, he wouldn't want it inside his apartment either. "How many do they grow in here?" There was so much vegetation in the room it was impossible to even estimate.

"The last time I read the visitors guide, it said the museum had five thousand different kinds. I haven't read it recently to see if they've added more." Slipping her hand into his, she led him around a slim tree and past a glass door leading into another exhibit. "We could come back every month and see different ones. That's one of the reasons I love this part of the museum so much. It's always changing."

If this room alone contained so many plants, how many filled the entire building? While Allison checked out a flower the color of the sky at sunset, he checked out the room on the other side of the glass wall. "What's in there?" Unlike the room they stood in now, the one next door wasn't filled with bright purples and pinks but rather various shades of green.

"They grow medicinal plants in there. We can pop in there next if you want."

At least those plants served a purpose, something he couldn't say about the colorful flowers around him now. "You pick. I don't know anything about this stuff."

"I usually go in there last. That and the desert room are my least favorite sections. Sometimes I skip them altogether."

Maybe he'd get lucky and she'd skip them today. His stomach might not make it if she insisted on seeing all the exhibits today. Already it felt as if something was trying to claw its way out.

"You should see it here at Christmas time. They go all out with decorations and they schedule concerts. Aunt Elizabeth and I heard a great church choir here in December singing holiday music."

Every time she mentioned her aunt, aka the First Lady, he pictured the woman who had stood near her husband when he took the oath of office. Unfortunately, that image only led to him questioning his own sanity. He had no business being with a woman whose relatives resided in the White House, yet there he was following her as she examined flowers, hoping she'd send him another of her killer smiles.

The sound of the doors sliding open grabbed his attention. With a tree and all types of leaves in the way, it was impossible to get a good look at who entered the room, but the high-pitched whine followed by a screech told him enough. Someone had an unhappy child with him or her.

"Time to go check out something else." Allison whispered the words to him, although she could've shouted and the other guests in the room wouldn't have heard her over the screaming little boy who had thrown himself down on the ground. "The Hawaii exhibit might be far enough away."

The kid had a set of lungs on him. "Unless that's in another building, I doubt it."

Another scream bounced off the walls, and he wished he'd packed the ear protection he used at the gun range.

"You've got a point. Let's go outside to the Rose Garden. We can come back inside later." She led him past the couple trying to convince their son to get off the floor and back into a hallway. "This way." Allison's thumb rubbed his palm, her skin warm and soft against his. The little gesture sent his gut into his boots.

Standing inside the lush garden, one could forget they stood in the heart of a city if not for the buildings in the distance. Unlike the orchid room, which they'd had to themselves until the screamer and his parents arrived, other guests wandered around the garden enjoying the scenery.

"This garden makes me think of hide-and-seek," Allison said as she looked around.

"You must have played a different version of hide-and-seek than me."

She nudged him in the side with her elbow. "Not because of the flowers. One of the gardens at my dad's house in Barrington is designed in a similar way. Derek, Alec, my cousin Sara, and I played hide-and-seek in it all the time. It had some of the best hiding places. Alec hid himself so well one day we got tired of looking for him and went inside. He ended up falling asleep. He spent five or six hours in the garden. Mom was furious at us for leaving him out there."

"He shouldn't have fallen asleep then."

"We tried that argument. She didn't buy it. Instead, she lectured us about how we were older and should look out for him," she said, stopping and looking around the garden.

"Something wrong?" He made a quick survey again of the other people around them then looked back at Allison.

"No, just taking it all in." She moved closer and wrapped an arm around his waist, and his heart did its little Jack-in-the-box routine again. "Anyway, I didn't get why she was so mad then, but now I do. We should've yelled out that we gave up or something instead of just going inside."

Whatever politic genes flowed through the Sherbrooke clan had skipped her, because the woman just could not lie worth a damn. She was uneasy for some reason.

He checked each individual gathered around them again. Everyone outside was either part of a couple or a small group, except for one person. Down by the concrete wall, an athletically built man wearing a black golf shirt, tan pants, and sunglasses stood alone. Dark brown hair hung below his Georgetown baseball cap and brushed against his collar. With his face bent toward a guidebook, it was impossible to make out any facial features. It didn't look like the guy was paying any attention to them or anyone else; still, something about the dude told Rock he didn't belong.

If she didn't want to admit something was wrong, he'd play along. "Who's older, you or Derek?" Addie had shared a lot of Sherbrooke family trivia with him before her wedding, so he knew Allison had a twin brother.

"Derek's five minutes older. He never lets me forget it

either." Her arm tightened around him as they turned down a different path. "He loves referring to me as his little sister because he knows it drives me crazy."

Rock checked out the dude by the wall again. He'd closed the book in his hands and was now looking at some roses nearby. He didn't know any guys who would come to a place like this by themselves to check out flowers. Maybe he was hanging out here waiting for someone. Or maybe he figured it'd be a good place to pick up woman.

"He's called me that more than Trent and Gray combined."

"Picking on a kid sister goes with being an older brother. Ask Addie about the things we pulled on her." A few of the more memorable pranks came to mind and Rock reconsidered. "Forget that. Don't ask her."

Right away, she let go of him and took a few steps away as she opened her shoulder bag. "No way. I'm going to call her now."

He wrapped his arms around her and pulled her against him before she had the phone out of her bag. "Later."

"Afraid she might give away some embarrassing secrets?" She let her bag hang by her side again and smiled. "Don't worry, I won't share anything she tells me with anyone else."

Her lips moved but the words floated past his ears. It was hard to concentrate on them when all he wanted to do was kiss her. So far today, he'd only gotten a brief taste of her, just enough to tease him and make him crave more.

"I'm sure—"

Keep it quick. Moving them behind a large bush, he pressed his lips against hers, cutting off the rest of her sentence. *Perfection.* Unable to stop, Rock applied more pressure and let his hands drop a little lower. *Mannaggia,* he shouldn't have started this now, but damn she tasted good.

Her tongue traced his lips. When he didn't respond, she sucked on his bottom lip. *Merda.* Did she have any idea of what she was doing to him? Already he was going to be incredibly uncomfortable for the rest of the afternoon. If he gave into what she wanted, he wouldn't be able to walk out of here.

Sliding his hands up her back, he pulled her away, ending their kiss in the process. "It might be safe to go inside and check out the other exhibits, or I can show ya what else I have planned for the day."

"I hope it involves food. The poor couple inside the orchid room probably heard your stomach over their screaming son."

He'd kissed all her lipstick off, revealing her naturally rosy lips. It might be the wrong place, but he couldn't keep from leaning toward her again for another quick taste. "Funny." Allison parted her lips to respond, but he silenced her with his mouth. *Lord, she tastes good.* Who needed food with her around? His stomach seemed to disagree with his opinion and took that moment to rumble loud enough for her uncle in the White House to hear it.

"Wow," Allison said, pulling away. "Let's get you some food before you pass out on me."

Rock had planned on letting her spend as much time as she wanted here. And while he'd seen enough of the place, guilt poked him for making her leave now. "If ya want to come back after lunch, just say word."

Her sapphire-blue eyes, Sherbrooke blue as the media called them, assessed him. "Nah, I think I've seen enough for today. We can come back some other time."

Thank you, God. "Let's go."

Since they'd ducked behind the bush, several more museum guests had spilled out into the garden, including the family they'd left behind in the orchid room. "Looks like our friends joined us. I wonder how they got him to stop screaming."

"Bribed him with ice cream." His comment earned him a raised eyebrow from Allison. "What? It always worked on me."

"I can't picture you rolling around on the ground because you didn't get your way."

"Left the rolling-around-on-the-ground tantrums to my

brother Tom, but my parents used bribery with ice cream more than once on me."

"I really hope I get to meet Tom soon so I can tell him you said that."

"He's got another three months before he's stateside again." And by the time Tom was back, he'd be gone for six months.

"Good thing I have a fantastic memory," Allison said, reminding him he'd never told her he was being deployed again in June. "Is Tom the oldest?"

He'd tell her about his future plans later. "Jon's the oldest. Tom's a year and half older than me."

They passed by the same guy he'd noticed earlier with the baseball cap, but now a woman with way too much makeup and not enough clothes, considering where they were, hung on his arm, not that he seemed to notice her. Once again, the guy's face was buried in his guidebook.

"What about your other brother?"

"Frank's only tens month younger than Jon. He's out in California at Camp Pendleton."

"Yikes, I thought my parents were crazy for having Alec eighteen months after they had me and Derek, but ten months? Your poor mom."

"Yeah, well sh—stuff happens," he said, catching himself. Sometimes he forgot whom he was speaking to.

"That it does," Allison agreed as they walked back into the main building and toward the main exit. "So what does the rest of the afternoon include?"

"We need to grab the lunch I ordered from DuPont Café, then head over to Bartholdi Park." Unfamiliar with the restaurants in DC, he'd done an Internet search for places close to the park. The fact the joint allowed customers to preorder takeout picnics had sealed the deal for him.

"Nice. Let's try to find a spot near the fountain to eat. Did you know it was created by the same person who did the Statue of Liberty?"

Until he'd planned this day out, he hadn't known the park existed, and he only knew it contained a fountain because of the picture featured on the web. "Nope."

"I love seeing it at night when the lights are on. It's nice during the day too, but not the same."

From the sound of it, she'd spent a decent amount of time visiting the area. Considering how much time her family spent in DC and her love of flowers, it didn't surprise him. "We can stick around if ya want to see it tonight." What the hell else they'd do in the city until then, he didn't have a clue. DC contained a lot of museums and cultural attractions, but he could only handle so much of that stuff in one day.

You'd do it for her, a tiny voice in his head, and not the one below his belt, whispered. *Cazzo!* He would. Somehow, in a short span of time, she'd become important to him in a way no other woman had.

"We could always visit my Uncle Warren and Aunt Elizabeth until it gets dark and walk back over." Allison pulled her smart-phone from her shoulder bag. "Do you want me to call and see if they're home?"

Damn, he couldn't tell if she was serious or not.

"I think he'll like you."

Gritting his teeth, he answered, "Up to you."

Allison exploded with laughter and gave him a nudge in the side. "I'm kidding, well about stopping in to visit. I do think he'd like you."

He relaxed his jaw. Meeting the Commander in Chief hadn't been part of his plan today.

"Let's decide later." She titled her face toward him. "Worst case, we can spend some time together at my house." Her sultry smile told him she had more than just watching movies in mind. He liked her plan.

∾

IF HER HEART beat any faster, it'd jump out of her chest and start dancing across the dashboard. It had more or less been doing that all day, but had doubled its efforts since they'd left DC and headed back to Alexandria. She only hoped it managed to survive the rest of the day and night. And what a perfect day it had been so far. They'd visited two of her favorite places in the city, but that wasn't the main reason she'd enjoyed herself so much. No, what made it great was the fact Rock had obviously put so much effort into planning their day. The Botanic Garden and Bartholdi Park weren't Rock's type of places. He'd taken her there simply because he'd guessed she'd enjoy it, and he'd been spot on.

With the first part of the day over, she intended to control the rest of their time together. For that, she didn't need any prying eyes or possible cameras. The memory of their kiss behind the rosebush surfaced and she bit down on her lip to keep from sighing. Despite standing in a public place surrounded by people, she'd been seconds away from pulling his shirt from his waistband and running her hands up and down his bare skin when he ended their kiss. She didn't do things like that. *Ever.* She avoided doing anything that might reflect poorly on her or the family. Unlike her brothers, she cared about what others said about her. Tearing a man's clothes off in the middle of DC would definitely earn her a boatload of negative attention from the media.

In the privacy of her home though, they could do anything they desired and not worry about photographers hoping to snap a juicy picture. And Allison knew what she wanted. The very thing she'd dreamed about every night now since the fundraiser. Rock wanted it too. He'd been a gentleman and not pushed for anything, but his kisses spoke volumes, as did the erection she'd felt pressed against her. Tonight, she intended to let them both have what they desired.

Her stomach flipped at the thought, and she adjusted the air vent, hoping her sudden temperature spike didn't show.

"You okay?" Rock's sexy nighttime DJ voice sent her body temperature up to a new all-time high.

"Great." *Don't look at him.* She'd never been great at hiding her emotions or thoughts. If he got a good look at her face, he'd guess in a second what she'd been thinking about.

"You look warm. Do ya want me to turn up the AC?"

"Um, sure." Shoot. Once again, she'd given herself away. "I'm a little warm." Unfortunately, no amount of air conditioning would help cool her off at the moment.

Colder air blasted out of the vents, causing her hair to blow around her face. Annoyed, she pulled it back and wrapped the elastic from her wrist around it. "What did you think of the park?" she asked while she watched him turn onto her street.

"Nice." He headed for the one empty spot on her entire street. A spot that didn't look big enough to fit a motorcycle, let alone Rock's truck. Somehow though, he maneuvered the pickup into the space on the first try.

"I'm a little jealous."

"Jealous?"

"I would've looked for a spot over on Washington Street rather than try to fit my car in this one. Parallel parking and I don't get along."

Rock chuckled. "It's easy. I'll teach ya."

Oh, she bet he could teach her a lot of things, besides parallel parking, and she hoped to start some lessons tonight. "Maybe some other time." Leaning closer, she kissed his cheek. "Come on, let's go inside." She didn't wait for an answer before opening her door and climbing out.

He wasn't touching her, yet she sensed him behind her as she punched in her alarm code. "Are you up for a movie?"

Reaching out, he pulled the elastic from her ponytail and ran his hand through her hair, making her scalp tingle. "Game for anything," he said, his other hand sliding along her jaw and to her lips.

Unable to resist, she darted her tongue out and licked his index finger. "Anything, huh?"

Leaning in, she kissed him before he could answer, and at the same time, she pulled the back of his shirt from his jeans and slipped her fingers underneath. The muscles beneath her hands flexed as she ran her palms up his hot skin toward his shoulder blades. Cotton rubbed against her back seconds before rough, callused hands touched her.

One of them moved toward the staircase first, although she wasn't sure whom and didn't care. Her leg hit the bottom step, and she lifted her foot. She didn't get a chance to put it back down. Instead, Rock lifted her and she wrapped her legs around his waist as he carried her up the stairs. As he walked, he continued to make love to her mouth, because to say he kissed her didn't do justice to what his lips and tongue were doing to her.

The bedroom door squeaked when he pushed it open, and she unwrapped her legs from around his waist, expecting them to come in contact with the floor. Rock's arms prevented that from happening. Although it went against every cell in her body, she moved her lips away from his. "This will be more fun if you put me down." She traced the outside of his ear with her tongue and waited.

Rock loosened his hold just enough for her to slide down the front of him. "You'd be surprised what you can do standing up." He gave her butt a squeeze before he took a step back.

She'd be a blazing inferno right now if human combustion were a real thing. Her insides were on fire already, and all they'd done so far was kiss. "Maybe you can show me later." *Okay, where did that come from?* She didn't say things like that. Of course, she didn't sleep with men she'd only been dating a few weeks either, yet here she was about ready to tear Rock's clothes off and pounce on the guy.

The corners of his mouth hitched upward and he undid the top button of her shirt. "Will do."

No doubt about it, the guy was a deadly force when he smiled. She watched his hands while he unbuttoned her shirt, anticipation building inside her. Already, her nipples strained against her bra and she ached to have him touch her.

He released the last button and pushed the shirt off her shoulders before cupping both her breasts and giving them a little squeeze. "Perfect size." He pulled the fabric down, exposing one nipple and took it into his mouth.

Holy wow! Pleasure exploded and traveled though her entire body. For a second, Allison gripped his shoulders and enjoyed herself; then she moved her hands toward the buttons on his shirt. Her hands shook a little as she undid the first button. When she started on the second, Rock pulled her other breast free and rolled its nipple between his fingers as she gasped.

"Ya like that." It wasn't a question but a statement, one she didn't feel any need to answer. Instead, she concentrated on getting the rest of his shirt unbuttoned.

The lips that had a moment ago been wrapped around her nipple kissed the side of her breast and moved upward. "You don't know how long I've wanted to kiss this spot." His warm breath spread over her already heated skin, sending another bolt of excitement to her core.

Looking away from his shirt, she watched him kiss the birthmark on her left breast, the one she usually forgot was even there. His lips lingered long enough for her to push his shirt off his shoulders before they came down hard on her mouth. With his shirt gone, she ran her hands up his taut corrugated stomach, enjoying the way his abs contracted beneath her touch. Reaching his chest, she brushed her hand over his flat nipples and started to reverse her path, the button on his jeans her ultimate destination.

She didn't get far.

The hands he'd buried in her hair moved, and before she could consider what that meant, Rock tugged down her leggings before slipping a finger inside her panties to touch her.

Two can play that game. Allison didn't bother with the button or zipper; instead, she slipped her hand inside his jeans and touched him.

With a growl, Rock pulled away and tore off his jeans and boxer briefs.

Can you say big? For a second, she couldn't look away from his erection. She'd been with men before, but none of them had looked like him.

Before she could really enjoy the naked view he provided, he reached for her bra clasp. Then he pushed her down on the bed and removed her leggings, which were still bunched around her calves. Starting at her ankle, he placed kisses up her shin and along her inner thigh. Sucking in a deep breath, she waited for him to touch her again when he reached the top of her leg. Instead, the weight of him pressing against her thighs disappeared.

"What's wrong?" Propping herself up, she watched him grab the jeans he'd dropped on the floor.

Opening the wallet he'd retrieved from a pocket, he pulled something out of it as he looked over at her. "Nothing." He tossed everything on the floor again and leaned over her. "Needed to grab these." He pressed a condom into her hand before tearing open the one he still held and slipping it on, his eyes never straying away from her face.

Good thing one of them was still thinking clearly. Protection hadn't even entered her mind when she'd come upstairs with him, and it should've. She was on the pill, but they weren't 100 percent foolproof, and she didn't have any condoms in the house. Rock was the first person she'd been with in several months and the only man she'd brought back to her house since she moved to Virginia. She'd have to grab some this week.

Rock leaned over and kissed her before he hooked a finger under her panties and pulled them down, tossing them over his shoulder.

Allison all but squirmed on the bed as he stood there staring at her. If he didn't do something darn soon, she'd have to grab him and toss *him* on the bed.

"You'd make a terrible poker player."

They were naked and he wanted to talk about cards?

"Your expressions give ya away."

Guilty as charged. "What am I thinking then?"

Rock gave her a wicked smile. "This," he said before he slipped a finger inside her, rendering her speechless for the foreseeable future.

~

SHE COULDN'T STOP from touching the pulse in her neck. The silly thing remained almost as out of control as it did when she finished the intense fitness challenge training class at the gym. Maybe she should give up her gym membership and have sex with Rock everyday instead. It was definitely much more enjoyable. No, enjoyable wasn't the right word to describe it. Incredible and mind-blowing were much better adjectives. At least it had been incredible for her. Hopefully it had been for him too, not that she'd ever ask him such a question. What if he said no? Talk about the ultimate in embarrassment.

Rolling onto her side, she propped herself up on her elbow. With his eyes closed and an arm tucked under his head, he appeared the most relaxed and easygoing she'd ever seen him. And since he seemed unaware of what she was doing, she let her gaze roam down his chest and over his stomach, her eyes drawn to the scar on his right side. She hadn't noticed it when he'd first undressed. Other parts of his anatomy had held her attention. "What happened?" she asked, touching the scar and tracing it with her finger.

Without opening his eyes, he covered her hand with his, making it impossible to move. "Bullet grazed me a few years ago. No big deal."

In her book, bullets and bullet wounds were a big deal, but

he said it as if he were talking about a piece of paper giving him a papercut. Maybe to do what he did, you had to think that way.

"It must have hurt a lot."

"Like I said, it was no big deal." He moved her hand away from the scar and up to his chest.

She got the hint. He didn't want to talk about it. "Can you stay tonight?"

At her question, Rock's eyes opened and he pulled her head closer to his face. "Definitely." His lips closed over hers before she could respond.

From the hallway, the doorbell chimes echoed, but she ignored it. The only guests besides Rock she'd had since moving in were Jake and Charlie. With a new baby at home, neither of them would be ringing her doorbell tonight. Uncle Warren and Aunt Elizabeth didn't do last-minute visits, and she didn't have any other relatives in the area. That only left some door-to-door salesman like the cable guy who rang her bell last week. No way was she getting out of bed for a salesman.

Rock pulled her on top of him, his hands moving to her butt, as the chimes echoed again.

"Do ya want to check the door?" He squeezed her ass before sliding a hand in between them so he could touch a breast.

"Nope," she said, her lips inches from his neck.

The faint sound of her brother's ringtone traveled up the stairs from where she'd left her phone in the foyer, and Allison froze. She didn't need to look. She just *knew* Derek was ringing her doorbell. And since he saw her car in the driveway, he was calling to see why she hadn't answered the door. *Darn it.* If she didn't answer the phone or door, he'd worry.

Scrambling off the bed, she grabbed her leggings and yanked them on.

"What's going on?" Rock asked, his voice both confused and surprised at the same time.

"Derek's here." She pulled on her shirt and at the same time tossed Rock's jeans on the bed. "It'll be easier if I just let him

95

in." *Man, oh man.* Of all the times for Derek to visit, he had to pick now.

By the time she finished buttoning up her shirt, Rock had his clothes back on too.

"Talk about déjà vu," Rock said as they walked downstairs together.

Allison paused. Did he make it a habit to greet all his girlfriends' family like this? "What?"

"I showed up at Addie's place to surprise her last fall. Ended up interrupting her and Trent like your brother."

Right now, she wished she were a little more like Trent. He wouldn't have been at all embarrassed. She shouldn't be either. They were all adults, and it wasn't her dad waiting to come in. Maybe she'd get lucky and Derek wouldn't suspect they'd been doing anything but watching a movie.

Don't give yourself away. Derek glanced up from his smartphone the moment she pulled open the door. "Hey, you. Come on in," she said, pasting on a smile.

Stepping inside, he looked past her at Rock and then back, a smirk on his face. "Bad timing, I see. Guess I should've called on my way over."

So much for a little luck tonight. "We were just hanging out." A little lie in this instance wouldn't harm anyone.

With a laugh, he hugged her. "Bull. You've got a rat's nest on your head and your shirt's buttoned wrong. You weren't just hanging out."

She looked at her shirt. Sure enough, in her rush, she messed it up. So much for playing it cool. Clearing her throat, she reminded herself again how much worse it would've been if her dad was there instead.

"Nice to see you again." Derek moved past her and shook hands with Rock. "Since I've already interrupted you two, do you mind if I stick around and visit?"

Oh, man, how she wanted to slap him. "*Mi casa es su casa,*" she said with a hint of sarcasm. "Let's go in the other room." She loved Derek, but the sooner they finished their little visit, the sooner he'd leave. "What are you doing here anyway?"

Derek put an arm around her shoulders as they walked toward the kitchen. "What, I can't visit my lil sister?"

"See what I mean?" She looked over at Rock, but he only grinned back at her. "Five minutes between us and he acts like it's five years." She rolled her eyes and turned her attention toward Derek again. "I talked to you two days ago and you didn't say anything about coming down."

"Decided at the last minute. Figured I'd visit you and then go see Jake and the baby. Then head home on Monday morning." Derek went straight to the refrigerator. "I didn't stop to eat on the way down. Do you have anything good in here?"

"Help yourself," she said, although there was no need. Before the move down here, Derek had always treated her apartment in Providence as if it was his own, so it made sense he'd do the same thing here. Of course, she more or less did that too whenever she visited his condo. "Where are you staying?" She already knew the answer to her question, but asked anyway.

"With you." He put the pizza she hadn't finished the night before and a sparkling water on the table and looked over at Rock, who'd sat next to her. "Unless that's a problem, lil sis."

"If you don't stop calling me that, it will be."

"Has she been this grumpy all day?"

"She was *very* happy until you arrived," Rock said, leaning back in his chair as if he hadn't just hinted at what they'd been doing when Derek interrupted them.

"Guessed as much."

Her brother's answer sent the heat in her face up to her scalp.

Derek pulled a slice of pizza out and smiled at her before he nodded in Rock's direction. "After I eat, I'll disappear for a few hours."

Were Rock and Derek really having this conversation?

"Much appreciated."

The groan slipped out before she could stop it. "Will you two please stop."

Her brother and Rock exchanged some kind of look she couldn't decipher, and she held her breath. *What are they going to say next?*

"I saw Trent and Addie on Tuesday," Derek said.

Thank you.

"I got the impression they know the baby is a boy. They both denied it when I asked. Have they said anything to you guys?"

"Got the same answer," Rock answered. "But I think you're right."

Allison listened as the men switched from one topic to another, the whole time wishing her brother would do less talking and more eating. The faster he finished eating, the sooner he'd be gone.

"Allison, you've got to work on that," Derek said, his sudden switch in topics jarring.

"Huh? What?"

"Not letting the world know what you're thinking." Her brother pointed a finger at her. "You're wondering how much longer until I leave."

Did she really give herself away that much?

"Told her she better never play cards," Rock said, offering his opinion on the subject.

Great, another one from the peanut gallery.

"She's better than when we were kids. We used to play a modified version of poker. She always lost. Couldn't bluff to save her life." Chugging the rest of his water, Derek pushed his chair back. "I'll see you guys later. Maybe around ten or so."

"Thanks for the warning, brother dear."

"Do you have a key I can use to get in when I come back, so I don't disturb you again?"

Nope, don't respond to that one. Allison grabbed the spare key she kept in a kitchen drawer. "Don't worry about rushing back," she said, dropping the key in his hand. "And if the alarm is on when you come in, the code is the same as the one I had at my apartment."

"Have fun tonight," Derek called out as he walked away.

Allison relaxed in her chair when she heard the front door close. She'd thought her brother would never leave. She still couldn't believe he'd alluded to the fact he'd interrupted her and Rock in the middle of sex so many times. Talk about embarrassing on a grand scale. The only way it could've been worse would've been if he'd actually walked in her bedroom. She owed him big time, but she'd figure out her revenge later. Right now, they again had the house to themselves and several hours to do whatever they wanted.

Reaching under the table, she touched Rock's thigh and moved her hand upward. She smiled, her own libido kicking all the way back on when she hit his zipper and the erection behind it. Slowly, she rubbed her hand against him.

"Upstairs now." He grabbed her hand, making it impossible for her to move it, and kissed her.

CHAPTER 9

HE WASN'T A VIOLENT PERSON. Really, he wasn't. But he had no other choice. He watched them kissing today at the Botanic Garden. Even now, the creep's truck remained parked outside her house. He'd seen her disheveled appearance when she opened the door for Derek. He knew what they'd been up to.

No man had any right to touch her but him. Yep, his mind was made up. The Marine had to die. Once that happened, she'd be his.

He knew the perfect person to contact too. *Kane*. A guy like him would know people. People who would take out Raimono and not ask any questions. Across the street, Derek exited Allison's house and drove away, and he slammed his fist into the wall. Damn, they were alone again. Blood trickled down his fingers, but he barely noticed as he pulled his second cell phone from his pocket. From memory, he dialed Kane's number and waited.

Soon, he'll be gone forever. And she'll be all mine.

CHAPTER 10

"I SHOULD'VE LET him come up again," Allison said, changing lanes on the highway again. She'd felt bad though. Over the past two and half weeks, Rock had made the trip from Dumfries to Alexandria several times. He never complained; then again, she doubted he complained about much. Still, it hadn't seemed fair he always went out of his way. Now, she wished she'd given in last night when they talked. Actually, they talked on the phone a lot, which surprised her, because Rock didn't seem like the type to have phone conversations on a regular basis.

"Relax and think about the night ahead." Doing that shouldn't be difficult. She'd been looking forward to spending time with him again since yesterday. As far as she knew, he didn't have any definite plans for them tonight, but so what? Unlike the men in her past, Rock never insisted they go out every chance they got. In fact, since they'd started dating, their only three big outings had been the hockey game, the Botanic Garden, and a movie. They'd stopped for dinner one night too, but right afterward they'd gone back to her townhouse. The other times he'd come up, they'd ordered takeout and just spent time together.

A good portion of the day, she'd actually fantasized how they might spend their time together tonight. Since she'd gotten on I-95 however, she'd been wishing she could lock herself behind her front door and turn the security system on.

When she left work and spotted the car behind her, she assumed it just happened to be heading in the same direction. There were a lot of office buildings around the Falmouth Foundation and it was five o'clock on a Friday. She'd assured herself it was just a coincidence when the same car followed her onto the highway. Lots of people used Interstate 95 everyday to commute to and from work. Just because the car had been behind her since the city didn't mean anything. The driver was probably heading home or off to meet someone like her.

That reassurance lasted until they merged with traffic and the same car stayed behind her. She'd changed lanes three times now, hoping the car wouldn't follow. Twice, the car behind her did the same. Had it followed this last time? *Only one way to know.*

Allison glanced in her rearview mirror then let out the breath she hadn't even realized she was holding. A bright red tractor-trailer with a large bulldog on its grill followed her, not the dark-colored sedan from earlier. She'd overreacted. *Again.* The car hadn't been following her. They had merely been heading in the same general direction.

A sharp cramp shot up her hand, and she loosened her death grip on the steering wheel. "I need to get control of my imagination."

The ridiculous thing had been acting up since January, but the silly bear and candy weeks ago had sent it into overdrive. So far, she hadn't received any more gifts, but she also hadn't figured out who sent the first one. She'd questioned the receptionist who'd accepted the present that afternoon, but she hadn't remembered anything about the delivery person except it'd been a man. Unsure of how to proceed next, she'd seriously considered contacting the police like Derek suggested. Each time, she convinced herself not to bother. The police had enough to deal with handling real crimes. They didn't have the time or manpower to hunt down her secret admirer, especially since the individual had only sent her a present. Sending presents, even anonymous ones, was not against the law, just unnerving for the person receiving them.

The red tractor-trailer passed her on the right as it headed for an exit. Immediately, she checked the cars behind her again. A white pickup now rode her bumper so close that if she stopped quickly, the driver would find himself in her trunk. Unfortunately, that wasn't uncommon for this time of day. And as infuriating as it might be, if it meant the dark-colored car from earlier wasn't around, she wouldn't complain.

The pickup drifted a little to the left as the driver spoke on his cell phone, giving Allison a good view of the cars farther back. She wasn't an expert on cars, but the dark sedan three vehicles back on the right resembled the car from earlier.

Is it the same one? They'd passed multiple exits since leaving Alexandria and she'd changed lanes three times. If it was the same driver, could it be a coincidence that they still remained behind her?

"In one mile, take exit twenty." The GPS directions forced her to watch the exit signs rather than the cars behind her, which was something she really should've been doing all along.

If someone did follow her off the interstate, should she still go to Rock's apartment? What if she parked and whoever drove the other car attacked her in the parking lot? Heading straight to the police station made much more sense. Too bad she didn't know where it was located.

Her stomach clenched at the sight of the white pickup truck and the dark-colored sedan following her off the exit ramp and right onto Dumfries Road.

"Turn left," the GPS said a few seconds too late as she passed the road she needed. Normally, she didn't rely on only the device's verbal instruction but also checked the map on the display screen. Thanks to the car behind her, she ignored the map and missed her turn.

The GPS repeated its instructions as the line representing her route changed on the screen to compensate for her error. A quick look in the mirror showed the dark sedan still behind her as she turned down the next street.

Unsure of what else to do, she pressed the phone icon on her steering wheel. "Call Rock," she said, thankful for whatever technology made it possible for her car and phone to work together. "Come on, answer." If he didn't answer now, she'd drive around until he did. No way was she getting out of her car without him around.

Rock ignored the beep of his cell phone. Ever since the pictures from the hockey game and another of them exiting Bartholdi Park went live in the media, he'd been getting texts from his buddies, all of them letting him now what a lucky SOB he was. Not that he needed any of them to tell him. However, a part of him did wish he'd thought a little harder before making out with Allison in full view of a camera lens. Having pictures of them kissing all over the Internet wasn't the best way to make a good impression on her father. She said it didn't matter, insisting her father wouldn't make any judgments about him based on some pictures. Regardless of her reassurance, he remembered his own reaction when he spotted a similar picture of his sister and Trent on the cover of *The Star Report* back in the fall. When he told Allison, she reminded him of Trent's playboy reputation and stated it had probably contributed to his negative feelings. He hadn't argued with her. People might call him a lot of things, but he wasn't a heartless playboy like the media had once portrayed Trent.

Oddly, he didn't disagree with Allison on much. Since the weekend they'd gone to the hockey game, he'd either driven up to Alexandria to see her or they'd talked on the phone. The only time they'd come close to really disagreeing had been last night. He'd promised to drive up once his interview with Elite Force Security ended, which was an event he still needed to process. She insisted this time she'd come to him instead. Rather than argue about something so trivial, he'd given in.

Right now though, he'd prefer to be in his truck driving instead of hanging around his apartment with Baxter and waiting. Somehow, driving helped when he had a lot on his mind. Tonight, he had a crapload clogging up his thoughts.

He'd expected his interview to be a meet-and-greet with Eric Coleman. The guy would do his best to convince him to join the company and become a glorified babysitter for any Tom, Dick, or Harry with deep enough pockets. Thanks to his conversation with Connor, he went into the interview knowing the company did more than just babysit, but he assumed that meant they also dabbled in some private investigating or something else along those lines. He hadn't been prepared for the truth.

To the world, Elite Force Security was just another pricey private security firm, which had been providing personal security for over forty years. However, some of its employees never worked as personal bodyguards. Instead, they worked as part of the H.R.T. or Hostile Response Team, a special division within the company developed almost twelve years ago. This division conducted the clandestine black-op assignments the Joint Chiefs of Staff, the CIA, and/or POTUS didn't want the US tied to, as well as hostage rescues. When Coleman dropped this bomb on him, his first thought had been that the guy was delusional. The idea of a secret paramilitary team running assignments for the government sounded like a plot for an action movie or some reality TV show. When no camera crew appeared and started filming, he accepted that Coleman was for real.

Now, he needed to decide if he wanted to sign onboard or forget he ever learned the truth about Elite Force's special division and go on with his life. The military was in his blood. Never had he doubted he'd join the military and serve his country. Except for his sister, it was just what Raimonos did. She was the black sheep of the family.

He never regretted his decision either. Unfortunately, the politicians often influenced the decisions made by those in charge, limiting the effectiveness of the military. From the sound of it, the orders H.R.T. received bypassed the politicians all together, making it able to carry out operations without all the bullshit and red tape.

Working for such an organization appealed to him on many levels. If he agreed though, it would mean keeping a part of his life a secret from everyone. The director had stressed more than once the level of secrecy all the men and woman on the team needed to uphold. In many cases, even spouses didn't know what their husbands or wives did. Did he want that type of life? He didn't have an answer and he didn't see himself reaching one tonight either, not with Allison around.

Allison. Now that was another case of there being more than what you saw on the outside. Most people probably looked at her and saw a beautiful woman who lived a life of luxury and did nothing more then get her nails done. He'd never admit it to her, but he initially had a similar opinion. There was a hell of a lot more to her than that.

During the past few weeks, he'd only scratched the surface, and the more he uncovered, the more he liked her. Perhaps it had been inevitable. She had taken him to a hockey game and a barbecue joint on their first date. Any woman who'd do that was a keeper in his book.

His favorite AC/DC song blasted out of his phone, causing Baxter to raise his head and look at him. Few people called him. Most of his friends and his older brothers preferred to send text messages. Only three people called him on a regular basis—his mom, sister, and Allison. If it was Mom or Addie now, he'd let them leave a message. A call from Allison he'd take.

Checking the number on the screen first, he grabbed the

phone and he hit the talk icon. "Hey, Allison. On your way?" He almost asked if she'd gotten lost. She'd admitted her sense of direction sucked.

"My GPS says I'll be at your apartment in three minutes. Can you meet me outside?"

The unease in her voice stopped him from asking why. Later, he'd find out what was up; for now, he'd go with it. "Sure thing."

"Thanks. See you in a few," Allison said before she disconnected the call.

Rock shoved the phone in his pocket. Allison's request made no sense, and neither did her tone of voice. He'd heard the same unease in her voice before too. He let it go on the other occasions; tonight, he'd get some answers, because it wasn't his imagination. "Outside, Baxter." Passing by the couch, he gave the mutt a tap on the side, sending him toward the door.

Several cars passed by before Allison's two-door coupe turned into the parking lot. When she spotted him, she waved before pulling in alongside his truck.

Stepping out of the car, Allison glanced at the road before looking at him. "I brought you a surprise," she said, holding up a plastic bag and walking toward him.

He ignored the bag and focused on her face. She was pale and her eyes kept darting to the road. Something or someone had spooked her.

"Let's go inside," he said, meeting her near the row of mailboxes and taking her free hand. What he wanted to do was pull her against him and kiss her. His gut told him she wouldn't be at ease until they were in his apartment with a locked door between them and the rest of the world. Her apparent unease didn't stop her from placing a kiss on his cheek, sending his pulse up a notch before she all but sprinted up the steps into the building.

"Hope you're hungry. I stopped at the Coffee Factory Cafe for lunch. When I saw the bear claws, I remembered you mentioning how much you like them," she said, naming one of his favorite pastries as he opened his apartment door for her.

"Thanks." Accepting the bag, Rock considered his next move. The head behind his zipper said to kiss her now and ask questions later. The one attached to his neck told him to get to the bottom of things first, because once he kissed her, they might not talk again for a while. "What's wrong?"

She gave him a forced laugh as she walked away. "Nothing is wrong." She slipped off her jacket and hung it on the back of a chair, a false smile in place. "How was the interview today?"

"Don't buy it." He dropped the bag on the table and crossed his arms. "Out with it, Ally." The more time he spent with her, the more he thought of her as Ally. However, he'd never called her that until now.

"My mom called me Ally all the time. Sometimes my dad would too, but not after Mom died."

Merda. She looked ready to cry. He preferred to avoid crying women. "It slipped out. Won't happen again."

"I like when you say it." Incredibly soft hands, hands he vividly remembered touching him in other ways earlier in the week, slid up his arms before settling on his shoulders as she pressed her lips against his.

The woman knew how to distract him and put off answering questions, but he'd get what he wanted before they moved from this spot. He pulled her hands away and took a step back so he could see her face. "Tell me what's going on. Why'd ya need me outside?"

"I thought someone was following me, but I think I was wrong. Right after I called you, the car turned and I didn't see it again." Her voice lacked its usual cheery tone. "Maybe it wasn't even the same car the whole time. Lots of cars look alike."

She didn't believe what she said. She wanted to, but her eyes gave her away. He saw the fear in them. "Start at the beginning."

Allison clasped her hands behind her back. If she didn't want him to see how they shook, she should've hid them sooner.

"When did you first see the car?" he asked when she remained quiet.

"Right after I left work. It stayed behind me all the way to 95. At first, it didn't bother me too much. Then, I don't know. I got this funny feeling, like something was up." She rolled her eyes as she sat. "Go ahead, say it. I know it sounds crazy. Feelings don't just come on when something is wrong."

"It's not crazy." Instincts and feelings had helped him too many times in the past for him to dismiss them as crazy. "What happened on the highway?"

"The car stayed right behind me. I changed lanes a few times and whoever was driving did the same. Even after I took the off ramp. That's around when I called you. I didn't want to get out of the car and be alone in case whoever it was followed me to your apartment."

"Smart."

"Then the car turned down another street." She played with her gold hoop earring and looked at him. "It could've just been a bizarre coincidence, right?"

Maybe if her last name wasn't Sherbrooke and her uncle wasn't the President of the United States, he'd entertain the idea it had been a coincidence or not even the same car the entire ride. Given the evidence he had though, he didn't buy it. "Has this happened before?"

The fingers on her earring stopped, answering his question.

"Ally?"

"The night of my accident, I thought someone was following me."

"Did ya tell the police then?"

"No. I thought maybe my imagination had run crazy. It was late and I was tired."

She was telling him the truth, but not the whole truth. "What else has happened?"

"Nothing really, but sometimes it feels like someone is watching me, especially after work when I walk to my car or if

I'm shopping somewhere. And then I got the silly bear and candy at work. Derek thinks I called the police and reported it, but I didn't."

"Ya should've." He would've told his sister to do the same thing.

"What am I supposed to tell them, Rock? Someone sent me a gift and that makes me uncomfortable?" A little aggravation replaced the fear in her voice.

"Considering everything else, hell yeah. There are some sick people out there who'd hurt you without blinking an eye. Or use ya to get to your uncle. Ally, you gotta do something. If ya don't want to involve the police, get a bodyguard."

"You have no idea how horrible and creepy it is having a bodyguard follow you around all the time."

The idea of some guy tailing his girlfriend didn't thrill him, but he couldn't do it himself either. "You need someone around, and I can't be with ya twenty-four seven. Give Elite Force Security a call. They're the best around here." Considering what he'd learned about them recently, he couldn't think of a better organization to keep her safe. But she didn't and couldn't know any of that.

"They are one of the best. My family's hired them before, but I just don't know." She stood and paced. "What if it *is* my imagination? I don't want some stranger invading my privacy because my brain's got its wires crossed." She paused in front of a window and rubbed her hands up and down her arms.

She wanted to play it cool, but he'd seen the same look before on many individuals. Deep down, she knew the truth and it scared her shitless. "How 'bout a compromise?" He didn't force women. Ever. They possessed their own minds. However, she needed protection, which meant this situation called for a little persuasion. "Get a bodyguard for during the day or whenever we're not together," he said, joining her near the windows and replacing her hands with his own. Despite the seriousness of the conversation, the close proximity intoxicated him. He wanted nothing more than to pull her so close he didn't know where his body ended and hers began. "And stay—"

Glass shattered and intense pain sliced across his upper arm. Without hesitation, he pushed her toward the floor and covered her body with his. Later, she might have a few bruises, but better that than the alternative.

"Don't get up," he ordered, reaching into his back pocket for his smartphone. "When I tell ya, crawl across to the bedroom." Located on the other side of the apartment, his bedroom was as far away as she could get from the windows. "Call 911 and stay there." He pressed the phone into her hand.

"What's going on? Why do you want me to call police?" She searched his face for an answer but punched in 911 as he instructed. "Did someone throw a rock through the window?"

She thought a rock sent him for cover. That explained her lack of freaking out. Too bad he needed her to know the truth. "Tell them shots have been fired."

Every ounce of color left her face, and if she hadn't already been on the ground, he would've feared she'd pass out. "You're safe. Just do what I said." He rolled off her and got into a crouched position. "Move. I'll be back."

Rather than follow his orders, she sprang to her knees and grabbed his arm, gripping the gash the bullet left on its way by and making him grimace.

"No. If someone's still out there, it's not safe. Wait and let the police handle it."

Considering her size, she possessed a decent grip and it took a little effort to remove her hand from his arm. "No time. Just do what I said, Allison."

"Please stay." Her voice shook, but she didn't outright cry.

He repeated ever curse word he knew in both English and Italian in his head and nodded. His gut told him the SOB who'd shot at them was long gone anyway. "Get in the other room." Rock took back the smartphone and hit the talk button.

When the 911 dispatcher answered, they only managed to get the words "911, where is" out before he interrupted them.

"Shots fired at Glendale Apartments," he barked out as he moved back toward the window and at the same time kept an eye on Allison. So far, she'd held it together and moved into his bedroom.

The dispatcher asked questions, and while Rock answered them, he pressed himself flat against the wall near the broken window and peeked outside. Nothing. Not a soul moved in the parking lot or on the sidewalk. Even the street remained empty. He'd expected that.

Across the apartment, Allison didn't speak. Instead, she chewed on her thumbnail and watched him from the bedroom doorway. The fear he saw caused more pain in his chest than the gash on his arm.

Keeping clear of the window, he moved back to Allison and wrapped his arms around her. She shivered against him as if she spent the last ten minutes on the beach in December with nothing more than a bikini on, but she never cried or lost her head. Other women he knew would be a hysterical, sobbing mess and clinging to him. Not Ally. She possessed a backbone. She wasn't going to let fear overtake her.

"Everything'll be okay," he said, tilting her chin up and kissing her forehead.

She nodded. "I hear sirens. The police must be here."

The knocking on the door seconds later validated her statement.

I'M SAFE. Rock's safe. She repeated the words, but the shivering continued. Someone had shot at them. A bullet had actually flown right past her. Her stomach rolled and her lunch threatened to leave her. *No one got hurt. Just remember that.*

"There's nothing more for us to do here," Detective Graves, the police officer who'd come inside to take their statements, said. "We'll check the casing we found outside for any finger-prints. Who knows? We might get lucky."

She didn't know much about weapons, but she'd watched enough movies to know the casing was the part of the bullet left behind after a gun fired a shot.

"We got the bullet too. That might provide some leads."

Yeah, she'd watched the police remove the bullet from Rock's couch. Considering all the damage a single bullet could do to a person, she'd expected something larger.

"I'll be in touch with you both. Here's my number if you need to reach me," he said, handing them each a business card. "Please don't hesitate to call."

Allison tucked the card into her pocket and watched the detective and Rock speak as they walked toward the door. With Rock's attention elsewhere, she dropped her head in her hands. The entire event played through her mind again. One moment, they'd been kissing, and the next, Rock tackled her to the floor, covering her body with his. A tear slipped down her cheek as a light bulb went on in her head. He'd used his own body as a shield. In a heartbeat, he'd been willing to sacrifice his own wellbeing for her safety.

Her heart expanded, pushing its way out of her ribcage and filling her entire chest.

"You holding up okay?"

Allison looked up. Rock sat on the coffee table, his forearms on his thighs, facing her. "So, so." How about him? From the moment he'd pushed her down, he'd stayed in control. Would he be offended if she asked if he was shaken up? The oddest things offended guys sometimes. *He looks fine.* The outside didn't always match the inside. "Are you okay?"

"Just a scratch." He touched the rip in his shirt. A rip she hadn't noticed until he drew her attention to it.

"Baloney. You're bleeding." If she hadn't been looking right at the wet spot on his dark shirt, she would've missed it. "Rock, you need a doctor."

"Bullet nicked me. I've gotten worse cuts shaving." He pushed up his sleeve. "Not even bleeding anymore."

A blob of dry, crusted blood covered the wound. It did look as if his body had the bleeding under control. "We should clean it. Maybe put something on it so it doesn't get infected."

"Sounds like you're offering to play nurse."

She'd gotten certified in first aid and CPR when she started working for the Falmouth Foundation. If Rock's injury was as minor as he said, she should be able to take care of it. "I'll try, but if I clean it and it looks serious or starts bleeding again, I'm taking you to the ER. Do you have a first aid kit?"

He gave her one of his panty-melting smiles before he sauntered away, distracting her for a moment from the fact a bullet had whizzed through the window not long ago. *Earth to Allison, come in, Allison.* She needed to think about his arm right now, not how good he looked both in and out of a pair of jeans.

"Should have everything ya need in here." Rock handed her a large, white first aid box and a wet towel before tugging his shirt over his head, revealing the toned body underneath.

Like a magnet drawn to metal, her eyes zeroed in on his hard pecs and then down to his six-pack. *Arm, take care of his arm.* Taking in a deep breath, she popped open the box and searched for what she needed. "Do you think Detective Graves's suspicions are right? That this was some gang initiation?" He'd claimed a similar incident happened the week before in Southbridge, a nearby town.

"Anything's possible." He remained still as she cleaned away the dried blood.

She heard the uncertainty in his voice. "But you're not convinced."

"You need a bodyguard."

"Rock—"

"Listen, will *you*?" He grabbed her wrist. "Hire someone from Elite Force Security for when I'm not around. Maybe see if they do surveillance too. If someone is following you, we need to know."

No doubt she'd feel safer with either Rock or a bodyguard around her at all times. "That'll still mean I have a stranger camping out in my house every night."

He ground his teeth and shook his head. "I'll stay with you at night."

"You're going to move in?" Considering how high-handed he acted, she should tell him to back off, remind him she could make her own decisions and she might not want a roommate. Under different circumstances and with a different man, she would. "You want to commute to Quantico everyday from Alexandria?"

"No."

Whoa, what?

Rock leaned closer and stroked her face with his fingertips. "But I will for you."

Her heart started its expansion ritual again.

"Deal?"

She smelled the cherry-scented candy on his breath when he whispered the word. Unable to speak around the golf ball lodged in her throat, she nodded. Her response earned her another smile and kiss, which threatened to burn her from the inside out.

"Okay. I'll call them first thing tomorrow and set something up." She turned her attention back to his wound. With all the blood gone, the gash in his arm didn't appear as bad as she expected. It still looked painful though. "You're right; it's not bleeding anymore. I'm still going to cover it up to keep it clean."

"You'll call now." He dropped his smartphone in her hand. "My arm can wait." Crossing his arms, he moved away from her. "And tell them you want Connor Anderson assigned to ya."

She'd dealt with enough stubborn men in her life to know Rock wouldn't back down until he got his way. Since she planned on calling them anyway, she guessed it made little difference if she did it now or in a few hours. "Fine, but after, I want to hear about your interview today." The bullet through the window had stopped him from answering her question earlier. "Do you have their number?"

Rock once again disappeared into his room. This time when he came back, he carried his wallet and a clean shirt. "Here you go." He held out a wrinkled business card and watched her dial the number. "You should call your family too."

Getting a bodyguard was bad enough. "I don't—" Someone answered the line, cutting off the rest of her sentence.

Since the family had used the firm before, it didn't take Allison long to make the necessary arrangements. While she still hated the whole idea, at least she already knew one of the guards they were assigning to her. He'd acted as her cousin Callie's personal bodyguard a few years earlier when the truth about her birth became public knowledge.

"All set." Annoyance leaked into her voice. "Let me finish up your arm." She reached for a bandage and tape. "Now it's your turn. How did the interview go?"

Rock's knees bumped hers as he moved closer. "Call your family."

If her father got wind of this, he'd be down here as fast as humanly possible, which she didn't need or want. "Not right now." Once her father found out, the rest of the family would too. She'd end up with a few brothers and perhaps even a cousin or two camped out at her place along with her father. She loved her family, but didn't need them moving in, especially when the whole situation was probably her imagination getting the better of her. Yep, in a week or so, she'd be able to get rid of the body-guards she hired. Getting her entire family worked up made no sense.

"Ally, if my sister were in danger, I'd want to know. My dad and mom would too."

He means well. She needed to remember that; otherwise, she might hit him over the head with the first object she grabbed. "There's nothing they can do. The bodyguards are arranged and

I'll have you around. Everything will be fine." *I hope.* "Please let it go for tonight." She focused on covering the ugly gash and hoped he missed the wobble in her voice. "Did the firm offer you a position today?"

Rock sighed hard enough to knock someone over, but he didn't press her again about calling her family. "They did."

"And?" Although Rock remained stationed in Virginia at the moment, she knew he could be deployed or transferred somewhere else. While that didn't change her feelings or desire to be with him, a position with a firm like Elite Force meant he'd stay nearby, making their relationship much easier.

"Gotta think about it. They gave me some time before they need an answer."

She secured the bandage with one more piece of tape and Rock grabbed the shirt he'd carried out with him. "Don't think so." She snatched the T-shirt away and tossed it aside. She'd spent the last thirty minutes looking at his naked chest and thinking about how it'd feel against hers. No way was he covering it up until she got what she wanted. The shirt landed on Baxter's head, but the dog merely lifted his head and gave it a shake before resting it on his front paws again. The dog had been sitting next to her since she sat down and he didn't look about to move for any reason.

Rock cocked an eyebrow. "What *should* I do?"

When he put it that way, what other choice did she have than to instruct him? "Let's start with this." With a little tug, she pulled her shirt over her head and unclipped her bra, Rock's eyes following her movements. Reaching out, she took his hands, and the Adam's apple in his throat moved up and down as she brought his palms to her breasts. They scorched her nipples and heat gathered low in her stomach. When he gave them each a squeeze, the heat slithered lower to between her legs.

"Anything else I should do?" Warm breath drifted over her breast as he spoke, and she bit down on her lip.

Oh, most definitely. "Touch me."

117

Rock's tongue traced her nipple, and then he kissed her collarbone while his other hand moved down her side. "I am."

"Not there." He was playing with her. She heard it in his voice. Well, right now, she wasn't in the mood for games. Grabbing his hand, she moved it between her legs. The heat of his skin seeped through the fabric and touched her. "Here," she whispered, closing her eyes. For a moment, he obliged her request. When he moved his hand, she opened her eyes. "What's wrong?"

Rock leaned toward her ear. "Waiting for my next order."

"We need a bed for what I have in mind."

CHAPTER 11

HE FOCUSED on clearing his mind as he watched the last police cruiser leave. He'd given Kane explicit instructions. He wanted Raimono dead, but he didn't want it happening in front of Allison. He didn't want the memory haunting her forever.

Either Kane failed to pass the message on to the lackey he tasked with the job, or the dumb flunkey had ignored his orders. From what he'd heard, people only made that mistake once. When Kane found out what happened here, he wouldn't want to be the punk he'd seen fire at the window before jumping in the beat-up Camaro and taking off. That was why he hadn't called Kane the moment the punk fired the shots. Ripping a guy like him a new one would only be detrimental to his own health.

Another bout of rage bubbled up despite his efforts. He'd seen Allison go inside. The shooter had too. The Camaro had already been parked near the sidewalk when Allison pulled into the parking lot. If he'd known who sat in the car, he would've done something, tried to stop the guy somehow.

He'd realized it too late. *There'll be other opportunities.*

Back in control, he pulled out his cell phone. Allison and Raimono couldn't be together all the time. He'd remind Kane what needed to happen. Then he'd wait. But he couldn't wait forever.

CHAPTER 12

MAN, she hated this. She couldn't even walk outside the building for a coffee without Connor following her. The man had been her constant shadow since he'd arrived at her house this morning. Actually, she'd had a shadow since Friday night, but one of them she didn't mind having.

Although not her original plan, she'd spent Friday night at Rock's apartment. Then on Saturday, he'd followed her home and stayed with her until this morning when he'd left for the base, but only after Connor arrived. Now she was stuck with Connor until Rock got back tonight. And lucky her, she'd get to repeat the entire process again tomorrow.

Yesterday, she tried to convince Rock they'd overreacted on Friday, that she'd imagined someone had followed her to his apartment. The whole experience had been like talking to a concrete wall. No matter what argument she made, he had a counterargument. In the end, she gave up, promising herself that if all remained quiet for the next few days and Elite Force didn't see anything suspicious, she'd get rid of the bodyguards. If Rock wanted to keep staying with her and commute everyday, he could. She liked having him close, and besides, he gave her some personal space, unlike Connor, the bodyguard now sitting outside her office door.

When they'd arrived at the Falmouth Foundation earlier, he'd insisted he sit inside her office. If she had to, she could deal with having a bodyguard in the building and even driving with him in the car, but she drew the line at him sitting across the desk from her. If he'd stayed in the room with her all day, she'd never get anything done.

It took some big-time persuading, but she'd managed to get him to stay just outside her door. Of course that meant the man knew when she left her office to get a coffee or even go to the restroom, and he insisted on going everywhere with her, which was something she'd found out very quickly this morning when she'd tried to make her usual ten thirty coffee run next door. The moment she opened her office door, he came to his feet. When she'd told him of her plan, he fell into step next to her.

She'd allowed him to accompany her to the café without an argument—after all, she hired him to keep an eye on her. Doing so would be impossible if he stayed here while she walked outside and to the next building. She'd even bought him an espresso and a muffin. However, when they returned and he tried to check the restroom before she went in, she put her foot down. Invading her privacy was one thing. Other female employees used the ladies' room though and they didn't need Connor or any other man walking in on them.

Connor hadn't liked that one bit. Only after she reminded him the receptionist would've seen any nonemployees go into the bathroom, had he conceded and stood guard outside the door instead.

The only positive thing, if one could call it positive, was that Jake had taken a few days off this week to spend time with Charlie and Garret, so he didn't know about the situation. He would soon enough. After all, a large, armed man had followed her into work and now sat outside her office door. No doubt Cindy, Jake's personal assistant, would tell him the next time they spoke. When he learned the truth, questions would follow. Hopefully none of that took place today, because she needed to get things done. Several grant proposals required her attention if she hoped to meet their end of the month deadlines.

Allison scrolled down and started on the next grant section, but two hard knocks on the door made her pause. *What can he possibly want?* Except for following her around every time she stepped out of her office, he'd left her alone to work so far today.

"Come in." The sooner she found out, the sooner he'd go back to leaving her alone—well, at least until she tried to make a break for the ladies' room again.

"Something you want to share?"

Phooey. Jake. So much for a little more time. "I thought you were out until Thursday." A little small talk never hurt anything, even if it did only postpone the inevitable.

"I was until Cindy called and said you had a guard sitting outside your door. Out with it. What's going on?" Jake stood on the other side of her desk, his arms crossed and his serious expression making him look like a younger clone of Uncle Warren.

"First, how are Charlie and Garret? Do you have any new pictures of him?" She'd answer Jake eventually. In the long run, what other choice did she have? Still, she didn't appreciate him barging in and demanding answers. He might be her boss at the Falmouth Foundation, but he wasn't her master.

His expression didn't change, but Jake ran a hand through his short hair. "Okay, fine, we'll do it your way. Everyone's great. Maureen and her husband are down visiting again." Pulling out his smartphone, he touched the screen before passing it to her. "These pictures are from last weekend when Sara and Christopher flew out."

Score one for me. With four brothers and a slew of male cousins, she didn't often win. She scrolled through the various pictures. Many of them were of Garret alone, but there were also a few of Garret with Jake's sister Sara and her soon-to-be husband, who also happened to be Jake's best friend, Christopher Hall. "He looks like you. Uncle Warren must be crazy happy. Two grandsons in less than a year." She reached the last of the most recent pictures, one of Garret asleep on Charlie.

"Allison."

"What? He must be."

Jake grabbed the phone before she could scroll through any older photos. "I answered your questions. Now out with it. What's with the armed guard outside your door?"

Looks like the reprieve is over. "It's nothing. He'll be gone in another few days." She didn't care what Rock or anyone else said. Unless someone at the security firm came back with evidence confirming she needed a full-time bodyguard, she'd be parting ways with Connor and Neil, the other bodyguard Elite Force assigned to her, soon.

"That's not an answer." Shoving the smartphone into a pocket, he sat and eyed her over his steepled fingers, a clear indication he had no intentions of budging until he got the answers he wanted. She'd seen both her dad and uncle strike a similar pose when dealing with their children.

When did Jake turn into a walking copy of Uncle Warren?

"Something made you hire a bodyguard. I can't help you, Allison, if you're not honest with me."

She loved Jake like a brother, but she didn't need or want his help. She had plenty of help already.

"Since I moved down here, I've had this weird feeling like someone is watching me. And a few weeks ago, I received a gift here with no name on it. At first I thought it was from Derek, some kind of silly practical joke."

"He told me about the bear and candy. He said you contacted the police."

"I changed my mind after I talked to him. It seemed silly to call them for such a harmless thing." Clearing her throat, she continued on before Jake could tell her what he thought of her decision, not that he needed to. His expression reflected his opinion beautifully. "Anyway, on Friday, I panicked when I thought a car followed me all the way from here to Dumfries." *And the bullet threw Rock's window completely totally freaked me out.* She kept the last thought to herself. Her cousin didn't need to know every minute detail.

"You're leaving something out. I don't know what, but there's something you're not saying."

Just call her cousin Jake the Observant. How he managed to know when people were leaving details out, she didn't know, but he'd always been that way. "Remember my accident in February?"

"Quit the stalling."

Dumb question, of course he remembered. He'd been the first person at the hospital that night, and she'd stayed with him and Charlie for the first few days afterward. "I thought I was being followed that night too. If I hadn't been paying so much attention to the car behind me, I might have avoided the accident all together."

"And you didn't bother to tell the police any of this, right?" Jake pinched the bridge of his nose. "Never mind. It's not important now. Okay, so you hired our friendly gun-toting buddy out there to watch your back. Have you called the police yet?"

"No." The single word had Jake opening his mouth. Before he could offer up a protest, she continued. "But if either Connor or Neil see anything suspicious, I'll call them right away. We both know they can't do anything without evidence."

"Until this gets figured out, come stay with us. If someone is stalking you, I'd rather you not be living alone."

Stalking. She'd avoided using the word and pushed it out of her thoughts now. Instead, she considered her cousin's offer. No one who didn't belong got into Jake's gated community, and if Rock weren't playing her temporary roommate, she'd take her cousin up on his offer for a little while. "I'm not alone. Rock's staying with me."

The corner of his mouth quirked up and he leaned his arms on her desk. "Yeah, Derek mentioned how well you two have been getting to know each other." Talking about the fact they were dating was one thing. Jake's tone made it clear Derek had shared more than just that information with him.

Heat started on the tops of her ears and spread to her face. Just because Derek freely discussed his sex life didn't give him the right to talk about hers, even if they were twins. The next time they spoke, she'd give him hell for sharing such personal information with Jake. "Derek's got a big mouth."

"Yep, he does, but your relationship's not a secret either. I've seen the pics of you and Rock on the Internet." Jake's smirk disappeared. "Don't worry; I didn't share what Derek said with anyone else. And I promise I won't."

If Jake gave her his word, he'd keep it. Now, could she get him to promise not tell the rest of the family about her armed friend sitting outside? Doubtful. "Can you also keep this little situation a secret? You know how protective Dad can be."

"Protective? Is that what you call it?" Jake chuckled, not that she blamed him.

Even before her mom passed away, her dad had been more protective of her than any of her brothers. After her mom's death though, his desire to keep her safe hit a whole new level. Even now, he occasionally acted as is she was a ten-year-old little girl who needed someone to take care of her. In fact, before her move, she'd sat through several heated discussion with him. He'd tried every argument he could to keep her from moving away from Rhode Island.

A little begging never hurt. "Please, Jake. Let's keep this between us for now, and if Elite Force uncovers anything, I'll call him right away."

Seconds ticked by. *At least he didn't say no immediately. It's a start.*

"You've got a Marine living with you and a bodyguard. You sound safe enough."

And here comes the "but." She heard it in Jake's voice already.

"Allison, you can't keep this from Uncle Mark. What if he stops in and visits. You know he and Abby are headed to DC, right? They're attending Congressman Paul Wickford's birthday party this weekend," Jake said, referring to a close friend of her dad's.

Damn it to hell, her brother Gray's favorite curse, popped into her head. If her dad and stepmother were that close, they'd visit and not necessarily call first either. Rock's presences she could easily explain. Thanks to the media, her father must know about their relationship. If her dad and Abby showed up, however, and either Connor or Neil answered the door instead, she'd have a lot of explaining to do.

"Fine. I'll tell him." *But only if I have no other choice.* Later, she'd call him and work on convincing him to let her and Rock visit him and Abby in the city rather than at her house. "But don't tell anyone else." If Jake shared the news with any of her brothers, she'd find them all at her door tomorrow.

ROCK ROUNDED the corner and ignored the slight twinge in his left hamstring. Considering the amount of weight he'd deadlifted this afternoon, the slight discomfort came as no big shock. Tomorrow, he expected even more, considering the fact today had been his first workout in days. The last time he'd exercised had been Thursday morning when he went for his morning run. He never took downtime like that. Even the flu the previous winter hadn't kept him from exercising. Staying at Allison's all weekend screwed up his routine, not that he'd do anything differently. She needed him, and he didn't intend on letting anyone hurt her.

She disagreed with him, of course. Again this morning, she'd insisted they'd overreacted on Friday night. She'd argued the car behind her had simply been a coincidence. His instincts said otherwise. They were never wrong.

Someone, the same someone who'd sent her the teddy bear, wanted her. He had no doubts the bullet through his apartment window was somehow related. He just didn't know if it had been meant for him or her. Stalkers did crazy things. The person may have decided that if he couldn't have Allison, no one else would.

Ice ran through his veins at the thought of a bullet tearing into Allison soft skin. *It's not happening.* She had a bodyguard with her during the day and him at night. She'd remain safe. For about the fiftieth time since Friday, he wished he could stay with her all day instead of the men she'd hired. His own responsibilities made it impossible. Maybe if they were married, he could get some emergency leave, but under the current circumstances, he'd have to trust Neil and Connor to keep her safe when they were apart.

"Hey, Rock," a familiar southern drawl called out to him as he reached his truck, and he saw Brayden Delray approaching. "Heading home?"

Close enough. "Yeah. You?"

"Not yet. My mother-in-law is here. She's not leaving until tomorrow night." Brayden grimaced. "Been trying to stay away from home as much as possible until she's gone."

"Still afraid of your mother-in-law?" Brayden had complained about his wife's mother even before they married.

"You've never met the woman. When she dies, she'll probably take over hell. Anyway, I'm headed to Shooter's for a beer. Are you interested?"

In the past, he'd join his buddy, grab a beer and burger, and then go back to his place for some television. Tonight, a much more appealing evening awaited him. "Sorry, I've got things to do. Another night."

"Right, things to do." Brayden wiggled his eyebrows, and Rock's hand itched to remove the knowing smile from his friend's face. "Laurie showed me the pictures of you and the

Sherbrooke chick together. Don't blame you for wanting to rush home."

"Have fun visiting with your mother-in-law tonight, Delray." He didn't care to discuss his and Allison's relationship with Brayden or anyone else.

"Let's plan for the four of us to go out together once the wicked witch leaves."

A couples' night out. He'd done those before with a few of the women he'd dated. "I'll let you know." He had nothing against the idea. What about Allison? Would she be open to spending an evening with his friends? Up until now, they hadn't added friends to their relationship. If this thing between them continued, it would have to happen at some point. And he wanted it to last. He'd come close to calling his sister crazy when she'd fallen in love with Trent so quickly. Now he was starting to understand, because somehow in a short period of time, Allison Sherbrooke had planted herself in his heart. Each day that passed, her hold on him grew. She hadn't said anything, but he suspected strong feelings existed on her end too.

"Do that. Enjoy your night. I'm sure you'll have more fun than me tonight." Brayden frowned and pulled open his car door.

After all the stories Brayden had told him about his mother-in-law, he didn't envy what was waiting for him when he got home. At the same time, anticipation at what was waiting for him forty minutes away had him wishing Alexandria were much closer.

When Rock squeezed into a spot in front of Allison's townhouse later on, he spotted her car parked in the driveway, but he didn't see Connor's car. The bodyguard wouldn't have left her alone. He had his orders to stay with her until he returned. So where were they? Before he left the base, he sent off a text message letting Allison know he was on his way. When she responded back, she said she'd be leaving work soon too. That had been fifty minutes ago. It didn't take anywhere near that long to get from her office to home.

She's got great protection with her. He'd insisted Allison ask to have Connor assigned as one of her guards, even though he knew his friend would hate the job. He had known the guy a long time and knew what he was capable of. Rock trusted Connor to stop at nothing to keep her safe. The only person he trusted more was himself. The reminder didn't stop him from pulling up her contact info and calling her.

"You beat me home," Allison said after answering.

Home. The four-letter word echoed around in his head, causing the roots Allison had planted to dig deeper into his soul.

"I'll be there in less than a minute. We're turning onto Cameron Street now. I made Connor stop at Cooper's Smokehouse, so I could get us barbecue for dinner. It took longer than usual tonight."

The dark-blue sedan Connor arrived in that morning passed him and parked across the bottom of Allison's driveway. Rock wasted no time opening his truck door. A thousand ants started their march across the back of his neck the moment his boots hit the pavement, and he started for Connor's car. A quick glance around revealed nothing out of the ordinary, not even a dark cloud in the sky. But someone had eyes on them. And they were doing a damn good job of keeping out of sight.

Rock reached the car as Allison closed the door. Without hesitation, she smiled and wrapped her arms around him. "I missed you." Despite Connor standing feet away, she kissed him.

Going home to an empty apartment never bothered him, but he could get used to coming home to a greeting like this every night. He enjoyed her lips against his for half a second longer and then pulled away. The ants on his neck continued their march. He needed Allison inside behind locked doors. "Let's continue this inside." Rock took the takeout bag she held and put an arm over her shoulders. "Anything unusual today?" He directed his question at Connor.

"Nice and quiet."

Let's keep it that way. "Good. See you same time tomorrow."

Connor nodded and headed back around to the driver side. "Hope you're hungry tonight."

He faced the street, his back pressed up against Allison's as she unlocked the door. The position allowed him to keep both eyes on the street and protect her at the same time. "Starving." Her keys jingled behind him, followed by a squeak as the door opened.

Stepping up, he entered the house and took one final glance around before he turned and closed the door. "What did ya get?"

Allison paused at the alarm panel and punched in her code. "Large orders of ribs, chicken, and coleslaw, plus cornbread. They'd just taken it out of the oven. I skipped lunch today. It's always dangerous for me to order takeout when I've skipped a meal." She turned and started up the stairs. "Start without me. I need to change."

Considering the snow-white blouse she wore probably cost as much as his monthly rent, he guessed changing was a good idea.

Rock grabbed plates from the cupboard and set them on the table then pulled the to-go containers from the plastic bag. The scent of warm cornbread drifted toward him, tempting him to grab a chunk, but he held back. He didn't dine at five-star restaurants, but he had enough manners to wait until Allison joined him. He hoped she changed fast tonight. He hadn't been kidding when he said he was starving.

While he waited, he grabbed a soda and popped it open. Beer complimented barbecue much better than any cola, but he didn't want anything impeding his reaction time. Allison might still think they were overreacting, but he didn't.

"You didn't have to wait for me." She dropped a kiss on his cheek as she passed by him. She'd changed out of her business clothes and into denim capris and a lilac T-shirt. "I'm having a glass of wine. Do you want one?" She grabbed a bottle from the wine rack near the back door. "How did I forget to lock this?" Allison stopped and turned the top deadbolt. "I need to pay more attention in the morning. I left my bedroom light on too."

"The ones in here were on when I came in."

"I don't usually forget those things. Having Connor around is messing me all up." Allison frowned and shook her head while taking a wine glass from the cupboard. "Did you want some?" She held up the wine bottle.

"Not tonight."

She filled her wine glass as she walked to the table. "Jake stopped in the office today. Cindy, his assistant, called and told him about Connor being at work with me."

He'd known it'd only be a matter of time before someone in her family found out.

"I also called my dad."

Something's up, Rock thought as he piled food onto his plate, because although she'd claimed to be hungry, she hadn't reached for a single rib.

"He and Abby will be in DC this weekend for a party. He asked if we could meet them for dinner before they leave."

Never in is life had he done the whole 'sit down and get to know you' thing with a girlfriend's parents. It had never seemed necessary. This time it did. Not that he looked forward to it.

He'd spoken a few times with Mark Sherbrooke at Addie's wedding, and each time, he'd come across as friendly enough. Back then though, he'd been only Trent's brother-in-law, not the guy getting hot and heavy with Sherbrooke's only daughter. That little fact right there made all the difference in the world. Or at least it would to him if he had a daughter.

"I told him Friday night would probably be okay, but I needed to check with you first." Allison's forehead scrunched up and her eyebrows came together. "Do you mind?"

"Depends. Will I need to wear a tie?"

"You're not funny." She huffed, crossed her arms, and gave him an evil eye, which rivaled his grandmother's.

"Whoa, are you sure you're not part Italian? Your glare would scare even Nonna."

She tried to maintain her expression, but her lips twitched.

"Friday night's fine, Ally." Rock reached for another rib and put it on her plate. "You better eat before I finish everything."

"Thanks. I know going out with someone's parent can be dull."

Considering he'd agreed to dinner with her father, she still sounded worried. When she cleared her throat, he knew she had more to tell him.

"He doesn't know about the bodyguards and stuff. I'm hoping they'll be gone soon. Please don't tell him."

He wished he shared her optimism. He didn't see the guards from Elite Force Security gone anytime soon, not until Allison's stalker made a mistake. No matter what she said, she had a stalker. And until the bastard was caught, he'd make sure she stayed unharmed.

"Please."

If he was in Sherbrooke's shoes, he'd want to know so he could keep his daughter safe, which was something he'd physically be able to do. He couldn't say the same thing about her father. He looked healthy, but that didn't mean he could stop the crazy SOB if he attacked. And honestly, was there anything more the man could do? She'd hired guards from one of the best firms in the country, a firm that did a hell of a lot more than just play babysitter, and he'd moved in with her. Unless Mr. Sherbrooke possessed some superhero powers, there wasn't anything more he could add right now. Telling him at this point would only make him worry and stress Allison out.

"Won't say a thing Friday." He'd reassess his decision if and when something changed, because the situation would change. Unfortunately, he couldn't predict when or how.

CHAPTER 13

HE WATCHED them embrace down on the sidewalk before Raimono said something to the muscled moron who'd driven Allison home. She'd hired some private bodyguard. Damn Kane's flunky. The shooting at the Marine's apartment had freaked her out. If the punk had followed instructions, he wouldn't have this added complication now. But it didn't matter much anymore. His plans had changed.

The memory of what he'd found inside her house today had the vein in his temple twitching and all the muscles in his body tensing up. He wished he hadn't gone in again this afternoon, but he liked visiting. It brought him closer to her. He'd spent hours practicing his lock-picking technique so he could go in whenever he wanted. Finding the spare house key in her kitchen drawer had been an unexpected bonus. He'd made a copy and than returned the original in case she ever went looking for it.

Today he'd made his usual rounds of the townhouse. He'd grabbed a bottle of sparkling water in the kitchen before checking the Internet in her office. He liked scrolling through the sites she visited. It gave him ideas of what she liked and what interested her. When he finished, he moved upstairs. He always left her bedroom, his favorite room, for last.

The condom wrapper on her nightstand changed everything. He'd known Raimono had spent the weekend; he'd seen him leave this morning. Until he spotted the evidence, he'd convinced himself their relationship hadn't progressed that far.

He knew deep down on some level Allison felt the connection between them. He'd seen the way she looked at him. Talked to him. In fact, he remembered every word from their last conversation in December. She only needed time to recognize her feelings for him.

Damn you. Don't you know you belong to me, Allison? How could you let him touch you like that? Spoil you like that?

Pushing away from the window, he paced. He would've made her happy, if she'd just given him the chance. Now, they both needed to die. Raimono first. This time he didn't care if she witnessed his death or not. And he'd handle it himself. He didn't want some dumb punk messing up again. Besides, he wanted the satisfaction. No, he deserved the satisfaction after what Raimono did. With him gone, he'd take Allison up to his house in Maine and show her what she could've had if she'd picked him instead. Once he finished with her, he'd get rid of her too.

First, he had a few more things to get in order. This weekend though, he'd get what he wanted. He'd waited long enough. Yes, he'd have everything he needed by the weekend.

CHAPTER 14

"CAN you teach me to use a gun?"

Rock's hands stopped on his belt buckle. "What?" It sounded like Allison said the word *gun*.

"I want to buy a gun and learn how to shoot it. I already checked. In Virginia, you don't need a special license to purchase and own a gun. So will you teach me?" she asked again from where she sat cross-legged on her bed.

"What aren't ya telling me?" They'd never discussed her views on gun ownership and she never commented on the pistol he often carried. However, Allison owning a gun made about as much sense as him owning ballet slippers. If her thoughts had turned in that direction, something had to have happened today, because yesterday she'd been ready to call Elite Force and get rid of Connor and Neil.

"I think someone has been in the house." She gripped her hands together and played with the heart-shaped emerald ring on her finger. "This morning after you left, I went to check my email before Connor and I went to the office. The browser was open. I always close the browser when I finish on the computer."

That wasn't much evidence. Her expression however said she had more.

"And you know how the deadbolt wasn't locked on the back door last night when we came in? I asked Connor; he said he checked all the doors before we left yesterday and it was locked. So how did it get unlocked? And the lights were on when we came in last night. The only explanation is if someone was in here after we left yesterday."

She made a damn good argument. If Connor said he'd checked the doors, then he had. "What about the alarm? It should've gone off if someone came in." He'd watched her turn it off when they entered the house. "Does anyone have the code besides you?"

"Derek and the security technician who came out to check the system when I moved in." She shrugged. "And I guess the woman who used to clean my apartment when I lived in Providence, because I used the same code here. But Francine doesn't know where I live. When I moved, I didn't tell her where I was going."

He doubted some cleaning lady from Providence would be breaking into Allison's house, but it didn't mean she hadn't sold the information, because someone else out there had the number. That was the only explanation if someone had entered the house and not set it off. "Are you positive no one else has it? What about an ex?" Mr. Teeth, the ex-boyfriend, he'd met the night at Siena came to mind. She'd mentioned how reluctant he'd been to accept their relationship was over. It wouldn't be the first time a guy had gone off the deep end when the woman he loved didn't return his feelings.

Allison went from wringing her hands to drumming her fingers on her legs. "Yeah, I guess him too. We were together a long time and he had a key to my apartment. But he wouldn't know how to pick a lock and get in."

He disagreed. With enough patience and practice, anyone could learn to pick a lock, even a guy like her ex-boyfriend.

"Besides, my cousin Leah said Charles is seeing her friend Miranda Bergman."

Her announcement didn't cross Allison's ex off his list, but evidently it did hers. For now, he'd keep his thoughts about Mr. Teeth to himself. "That it? Nobody else?"

"Nope."

Although unlikely, someone could have guessed the number. "First, lets change the code. Then we're calling the cops."

Allison's lips parted, and he just knew an argument was about to follow.

"Sorry. It's time we get 'em involved. If someone is coming into the house, they need to be in the loop."

Her sigh almost knocked him over. "You're right. I know you are. I just hate calling them."

The sadness and fear in her voice melted into his heart, becoming a part of him. "Don't worry, Ally. I won't let anything happen to ya. Promise. Soon, we'll get the bastard stalking you."

Her smiled wobbled, but she didn't cry or give any other indication of the fear he knew she felt. "We'll do our first gun lesson after we call the cops." Rock grabbed her hand and pulled her up. "Do ya know how to change the alarm code?"

"The user's manual is in my desk. The technician who came out changed it for me but said it was easy if I needed to do it again."

"It's usually easy."

They grabbed the manual from the office and trekked down to the basement. Although a different model than the system his parents had, the directions for changing a code were the same. "What's the code now?" Rock asked, opening the control box mounted on the wall. In order to make any changes, they had to enter the current code first.

"0723."

"Your birthday is your alarm code? Didn't the tech tell you not to use a number like that?" *Mannaggia*, anyone with a computer and Internet access could find her code.

"He said to pick four numbers. So I did. I never told him it was my birthday."

Damn idiot. "Pick four new numbers. Don't use a relative's birthday or part of your social security number. The best alarm codes and passwords are random."

"Four random numbers, huh?" She nibbled on her thumbnail while she thought. "How about 0325."

Rock repeated the number in his head. "Sounds like a date."

"I know. You said it couldn't be a birthday. It's not. Besides, I have good memories of that date."

Whatever. If she wanted some random date for a code, he'd let it go. He punched in the new number, but something about it bothered him. "Why March 25th?"

A corner of her mouth twisted upward and she sighed.

Rock rolled the date around in his head. He cringed when it came to him. "The hockey game." How'd he forget that date?

She gave him a poke in the shoulder. "You almost found yourself on the couch tonight, Captain Raimono."

"Nah, you'd never send me there. You'd miss this too much." Rock pulled her against him and pressed a hard, hot kiss on her lips. She opened for him right away and her tongue slipped into his mouth, again showing him that her passion rivaled his.

Not now. He couldn't make love to her in a cold basement. If he kept kissing her like this, he'd forget why and lower her to the rough concrete floor then strip her naked. "Ally." His voice echoed off the walls. "We still need to call the cops, and you wanted a gun lesson. We gotta stop and get those things done."

She paused, her lips pressed against his neck. Then she exhaled, her breath a warm whisper across his skin. "Right. I forgot. My phone's upstairs. Do we need to go somewhere special for the gun lesson?"

She was stalling. No doubt about it. Allison could stall all she wanted. Nothing would change his mind about getting the cops involved now. Rock shifted back. Her body pressed against his made thinking difficult. "Today, we're goin' to review gun safety and stuff, so we can do it in the kitchen. If we have time

Wednesday or Thursday, I'll take you to the range for some actual shooting. Come on upstairs. You've got a call to make."

ALLISON WISHED she knew more swear words. None of the ones in her vocabulary did justice to the current situation. A stalker. She had some crazy person following her around, breaking into her house, going through her things, and even taking the time to use her computer. She'd read about such things happening, but she had never dreamed it'd happen to her.

Before her talk with Connor this morning, she'd written off everything as mere coincidence. She'd kept telling herself her imagination had been overreacting and Rock was being overprotective. When Connor confirmed the deadbolt on the back door had indeed been locked when they left for the office, she'd realized she could no longer deny all the evidence. While she may have forgotten to turn off a light or two, Connor would never forget to lock a deadbolt before they left. And now the police were about to get involved and make the situation even worse.

Out in the foyer, she heard Rock's voice as he greeted the officers the department sent over. When the doorbell rang, he'd insisted he answer even though they were expecting officers. She'd never had a boyfriend so protective and concerned for her safety. Having him around so much was the only bright side to this whole terrible situation. Even before the day the bullet flew through his window and he protected her without a thought to his own welfare, she'd suspected she'd loved him. Everyday since then had only reinforced her belief. Best of all, she knew he cared about her. No one acted the way he did if they didn't care deeply.

"She's in here." Rock's voice grew louder as he led the police toward the living room where she waited.

Two men entered the room behind Rock, and her immediate thought was *talk about an odd couple*. Both men appeared to be close in age and were dressed in a similar fashion. However, that was the only thing they had in common. While both appeared fit, one of the officers had to be close to seven feet tall, because he towered over Rock, while the other gentleman wasn't much taller than her. And while the shorter man didn't have a single wrinkle on his face, he also didn't have any hair on his head—unlike his partner, who had short, dark hair and a neatly trimmed beard.

"Good afternoon, Miss Sherbrooke. I'm Detective Wilson, and this is my partner, Detective MacLean," the taller of the two men said, extending his hand toward her.

"Nice to meet you. Please sit."

Both men took seats opposite her on the sofa while Rock sat next to her and reached for her hand.

"Miss Sherbrooke, on the phone you said someone has been following you. How long have you suspected this?" Detective Wilson said, getting right down to business.

"Since the first week in February." *Talk and get it over with*, Allison thought before telling him everything about the night of her car accident.

The detective asked her numerous questions about that night, and then they asked what other events made her believe she had a stalker.

"Have you received any gifts or strange phone calls?" Detective MacLean asked, taking over the questioning.

"I guess you might call them strange. I've gotten some calls where no one talks, but I can hear them. And I did get one gift at work. A bear with candy was delivered. The card didn't have a name on it."

"Do you still have it? Or know where it came from."

"Sorry, no. I threw it away, Detective. The card didn't have a store name on it either, and the receptionist at work didn't remember anything about the delivery person when I asked."

Across from her, Detective MacLean frowned and jotted

something down on his notepad. "You mentioned someone has been in your house. Can you tell us more?"

A shiver skated down her spine and she shook. Rock squeezed her hand before he released it and put an arm over her shoulders, pulling her close. While the gesture didn't change the situation, it did stop the trembling as the warmth from his body seeped into hers. More than anything, she wanted to snuggle closer and stay there forever. The two detectives in the room kept her from doing anything more than enjoying the sense of security Rock provided.

"When we came home yesterday, I noticed the deadbolt on the kitchen door was unlocked." Allison filled the two men in on every thing from her conversation with Connor to the fact that she found her internet browser open when she went to use her computer. In response, they began with the same question as Rock—who else knew her alarm code? And just like Rock, they immediately mentioned her ex-boyfriend as the possible stalker.

"Detective MacLean, I've known Charles Perkins for a long time. We share mutual friends and I know he's moved on. He'd never do something like this. It's not him."

Both detectives exchanged an unconvinced look with Rock.

"We can check for fingerprints, but there's a good possibility you smudged any the intruder may have left. That's assuming he didn't use gloves." Detective Wilson spoke up this time. "Have you already changed the alarm code?"

"Did it before we called ya," Rock answered. So far, he'd remained on the quiet side. The only time he'd spoken had been when she told the detectives about the shooting at his apartment.

"Under the circumstances and considering who your family is, you shouldn't be living alone, Miss Sherbrooke. I recommend you either have your bodyguards here around the clock or stay with someone."

"Detective Wilson, she's not alone. I'm here."

The detective's expression didn't change, but he nodded and added the information to his notes. "I suggest installing some surveillance cameras. I'm surprised the security company that installed your system didn't recommend them, considering your uncle is the President."

"The system was here when I moved in. The company who verified it worked properly suggested I upgrade and add some cameras, but I haven't gotten around to it yet." At the time, upgrading seemed low on her priority list, and adding cameras was just another thing to make her different from her neighbors. Already, her family name and list of relatives did that enough.

"We'll look into it tomorrow," Rock answered before she said anything.

"Is there anything else we should know? Even what seems like an insignificant detail might be helpful," Detective Wilson said.

"I've told you everything."

Detective Wilson closed his notebook. "It'll take a while to dust for fingerprints. Let me get the gear from the car, and we'll get started. We'll also need to search the entire house. It's not unheard of for a stalker to hide in an attic or a crawl space."

Even Rock's warmth couldn't prevent the tremor that went through her body when he mention the possibility her stalker had been living in the house all this time.

"It's gonna be okay," Rock whispered in her ear.

Oh, how she wished she shared his confidence right now. "Please do whatever you need, Detective Wilson. And if you need something, just ask."

"We appreciate it, Miss Sherbrooke," he said before he looked in his partner's direction. "Be right back, Liam."

HE DIDN'T LIE. It took forever. Allison watched Rock close and lock the door behind the two detectives. When they'd arrived, the sun had remained on the horizon. Now, a full moon hung in the sky.

"Still want a lesson, or do ya want to wait?"

What she wanted was to wake up from this terrible dream, but since that wasn't an option, she nodded. "The sooner the better."

Rock cupped her face and looked her in the eye. "Nothing is going to happen to ya. I won't let it. Don't forget that," he demanded in a voice that left no room for argument. "Come on, let's go in the kitchen."

I love you. More than anything, she wanted to say the words. He deserved to know how she felt about him. If she told him now though, would he believe her, or would he think she only thought she loved him because of everything going on? They hadn't known each other long. He might not believe two people could fall in love so quickly. *Wait for a better time. Tell him when there is not some crazy person breaking into the house and following you around.*

She watched him pull the pistol from his holster and place it on the table. She didn't have anything against weapons. They served a purpose. She'd just never had any need or desire for one. The events of the past few months made her reconsider that. Still, she couldn't believe she stood in her kitchen about to have her first gun lesson.

"First rule and, according to my dad, the most important one: always treat any gun you come across as loaded. Second rule: don't touch the trigger unless you intend to shoot. Third rule: never point at something you don't want to shoot."

Allison nodded in agreement. He hadn't asked a question, but it seemed like the thing to do.

"There are a lot of different models, but the basics are the same." He picked up the dull black pistol again. "Unless it's a revolver, bullets are held in a magazine. The number of bullets in a magazine will vary depending on the size of the gun and the bullet." Rock pointed to a tiny little button not far from the trigger. "This is the magazine release. It lets you take the magazine out. Every gun has one, but they're not all in the same place." He handed her the magazine.

The weight of it and the knowledge of what it contained sent a shiver up her arm.

"This one holds seventeen rounds. Then you got the one in the chamber." He racked back the slide and another bullet dropped onto the table. "Don't assume a weapon is safe just because it doesn't have a magazine. As long as there is one in the chamber, it can fire." Next, he pointed to the black square bumps on the top of the gun. "These are your sights. You use them to line up your shot."

One by one, he explained each part of the weapon. By the time he finished, several components were on the table and she hoped he didn't ask her to put it back together. While she listened and watched everything he did, she'd never get the thing in working order again. Perhaps after he demonstrated another four or five times, but not tonight.

"Questions?" Rock picked up what he'd called the frame and started reassembling the pistol.

Yep, she had some of those. One certain one bugged her the most. "How do you turn off the safety?" In books, it always said the character switched off the safety before firing. She'd paid attention. He'd never mentioned or pointed to a safety.

"This one doesn't have a safety you turn off." He made quotation marks with his fingers when he said turn off. "It's got a passive safety system. Pressing the trigger deactivates all of the safeties. As long as you don't press the trigger, the gun can't go off even if you drop it out of a helicopter. But some weapons have manual safeties you need to turn off before you shoot. I'll show you some different models later."

"Which is better?"

Rock finished reassembling the gun but didn't slide the loaded magazine back into it. "It comes down to personal preference. I don't like the manual safeties. In a fire fight, it's just one more thing to think about."

"But doesn't that makes it less safe?"

"Not if you remember the rules. But like I said, it's personal preference." He held out the unloaded weapon. "The grip on this is going to be too big. Addie shoots something smaller and your hands look about the same size as hers."

"Addie shoots?" Her sister-in-law had never mentioned she knew anything about guns, but then why would she?

"Hell yeah, and probably better than either of those two detectives who were here. My dad taught us all how. Even my mom. He wanted us safe around weapons."

She wondered what other unique skills her sister-in-law had. Allison accepted the gun and wrapped her hands around the grip. "I thought it would be heavier."

"This one's made mostly of plastic, so it's light. If it had a magazine in it, you'd notice a difference in weight."

She thought they only made toy guns out of plastic. Obviously, she had more to learn than she thought.

"Forget what you've seen in movies. It's best to keep two hands on the gun. Yeah, sometimes you can't and you need to compensate, but I want you to always keep both hands on the grip. And keep your finger off the trigger until you're ready to shoot." He repositioned her hands the way he wanted them. "We'll go over this more when we get to a range, but let's talk about firing stance. There are three basic ones."

By the time Rock finished his lesson an hour later, Allison's head spun from all the information he gave her. She'd thought all you had to do was point and shoot. Now she realized just how naïve her belief had been. She still had more to learn, but at least she had some basic knowledge. That was more than she'd had a few hours ago. She hoped she never needed to use any of it.

CHAPTER 15

HE WATCHED the two men get into their vehicle. Even though they didn't wear uniforms, everything about them from the way they walked to the car they drove screamed cop. Of course it helped that Detective Wilson was so tall. Thanks to the man's height, he was easy to remember and identify. He didn't know the other detective's name, but he'd find out. Having friends in the department came in handy.

Why had she called them tonight? He understood why she'd hired the bodyguard who'd stuck by her side all day yesterday and today. The shot through Raimono's window scared her. She had no way of knowing it wasn't intended for her. If she knew the truth, she wouldn't have invited him into her house. No, she'd want him as far away from her as possible.

But she didn't know the truth, which meant, thanks to the punk's screw-up, he had bodyguards now to contend with. He hoped Zane had made the punk suffer for his mistake at Raimono's apartment.

The sedan drove away and he again wondered why she'd contacted them. She didn't know he'd been in the house. He was too good for that. He locked up when he left and returned anything he touched back to its original place. He even took his empty water bottle with him. No, it wasn't possible she knew he'd been making periodic visits to her house since February. Had someone else broken in? Burglaries didn't happen often in this area, but they did occur. A robbery would account for a visit from the police. A break-in would also mean the police would look for fingerprints. *Good thing I always wear gloves.*

A robbery didn't seem right. She did have an alarm system, even if it was on the older side. An average lowlife breaking in would've tripped it, and the place would've been swarming with cops much earlier.

Damn, he didn't have a single answer. He hated not having answers. Answers meant control and power. He needed both. Tomorrow he'd pump, Kitty, his friend in the department for an explanation. Until then, he'd focus on his plans for the weekend.

He smiled at the mental image of Allison's Marine on the ground, his shirt bright red as his blood drained from a bullet hole in his chest. He pictured himself carrying her with a blade pressed up against her neck as she kicked and screamed over her dead lover's body. In his mind, he showed her what happened when a woman let someone else touch what belonged to him. The mental image alone made him hard.

He could hardly wait.

CHAPTER 16

"Nooo." *The faceless lunatic only laughed and pulled Allison closer. Light reflected off the blade he held as the knife moved closer to the artery in her neck. He had to get to her. Rock tried to run, but his boots sank into the cement. Across the parking lot, Allison's stalker whispered something in her ear and kissed her cheek. Bile rose up in his throat and he yanked his feet from his boots and started running toward them.*

"She belongs to me!" the stalker shouted.

Rock ignored him and looked at Allison. Tears streamed down her face, but she remained silent.

"Say goodbye, Allison," the stalker ordered, as he slid the blade along her neck, causing droplets of blood to appear.

His feet slowed, and no matter how hard he tried, he couldn't get them to move any faster.

"I love you!" Allison shouted, seconds before the stalker plunged the blade into her neck. Blood flowed down her skin and she crumpled to the ground before he reached her. At the same time, the man who'd held her captive vanished, his terrible laugh ringing in the air.

Rock dropped to his knees and pulled her close. Warm blood covered his hands as he tried to stop the bleeding.

"Ally!" he shouted out as his eyes popped open. The soft hair and warm breath against his chest reassured him Allison remained safe. It'd only been a nightmare. One similar to the dream he'd had the previous night. In that one though, the stalker hadn't killed her. Instead, he'd disappeared with her.

Just a dream, idiot. Nothing's going to happen to her. He repeated the mantra to himself again. Slowly, his breathing returned to normal, but the fear clawing at his heart remained.

Reaching over, Rock grabbed his phone on the nightstand and checked the time. Not even two o'clock yet. Great, he had another two hours to lie here and stare into the darkness. He shifted in bed and folded an arm behind his head. He'd suffered from the same problem for the past three nights, and each night it got worse. Unless the cops caught Allison's stalker soon, he'd not be sleeping at all. His lack of sleep wasn't the only reason they needed to catch the bastard soon. Each day that passed brought him closer to June fifth, the date of his deployment. The idea of leaving her was difficult enough, but he didn't know how he'd manage to do it if she remained in danger.

Allison's soft hair brushed against his chest as she snuggled closer. Even though she moved, he knew she remained asleep. He envied her. *She sleeps like the dead.*

He cursed himself. The last two words he wanted together were Allison and dead. *She's a sound sleeper.* Each morning this week, he'd managed to get up, shower, and dress, and still not disturb her. Only when her own phone alarm went off did she wake up, and even then she took her sweet time getting out of bed. It was a good thing she didn't live far from work. If she had a long commute everyday, she'd never get there on time.

Bits and pieces of his dream pushed their way into his thoughts. *"I love you!"* she'd shouted at him. It'd only been a dream, but the words still filled him with hope. She cared about him. He didn't doubt it. But she'd never actual mentioned love. Did she love him? She wanted him to meet her dad and step-mother. That meant something. But would she be willing to wait for him to come back? A woman like her could have anyone with the snap of her fingers whenever she wanted.

I could make this my last deployment. With everything else, he'd not considered the offer from Elite Force Security, and they wanted an answer. Eric Coleman had called him Tuesday looking for a yes or no. He'd been disappointed when Rock told him he didn't have one yet. However, after he'd explained the situation, the director agreed to give him until the end of the month.

He'd worry about the job offer later. No matter how their relationship turned out, right now he had a job to do. He needed to keep the woman he loved safe.

Rock kissed her forehead and tried to push away the unease inside him. Everyday, it grew more and more. Soon, something would happen. His gut said the stalker would make his next move within a few days. This time, the SOB wouldn't just send a teddy bear or sneak into her house either. What if he wasn't around when the bastard struck? Both her bodyguards knew what they were doing, and he'd trust Connor with his own life. But this wasn't his life in jeopardy. Allison needed him. Unfortunately, he couldn't stick by her side twenty-four seven. They both had responsibilities.

Allison bolted upright next to him, and he switched on the bedside light, all thoughts of the stalker put on hold.

"Ally?" She looked at him. Her face matched the bright white bed sheets. "You're safe." Even without an answer, he knew she'd had a nightmare.

"Sorry for waking you up."

"You didn't." He pulled her back down and held her. She shivered against him and he mentally cursed the SOB who stalked her. "I've been awake for a while."

"Sorry."

"Not your fault. Just got stuff on my mind."

"I don't ever have nightmares." She moved closer and slipped her leg between his. "I've never been so scared before."

Anger toward the unknown bastard had Rock grinding his teeth together. "Don't be. I promised you'd stay safe, remember? I don't make promises unless I intended to keep 'em." Allison didn't need to know about the fear he'd woken up feeling.

"It's not only that I'm afraid of getting hurt. What if this crazy person tries to hurt *you*?" Allison sat up and faced him, her worry written on her face.

Her expression stole all words from his mind. Once he regrouped his thoughts, he pushed up into a sitting position. "You've got nothing to worry about."

"You're not Superman."

"I'm a Marine. It's better."

"Stop joking around, will you." She punched the bed before poking him in the chest. "I'm serious, Rock. I love you. Nothing can happen to you."

He grabbed her wrist and pulled. "Stop worrying." Unable to resist, he gave her a quick kiss. "You trust me, right?" He gave her enough time to nod before he continued on. "I'm not gonna let some sicko hurt you. And nothing's going to happen to me. Got it. I love you too damn much." He kissed her again. When he tried to pull away and speak, she pushed her body against him.

"Instead of just saying it, show me." She whispered the words against his ear. Leaning back, she pulled off her T-shirt.

He didn't need any further orders.

"WHAT TIME TONIGHT?" Rock poured them each a cup of coffee before he flipped the omelet he'd started. He offered to make Allison one too, but she'd opted for yogurt and fruit instead, like she had every morning he'd been there.

"About six thirty. And we're meeting them at Siena. They're going to stop and visit with Charlie and the baby this afternoon, so it makes more sense to meet around here instead of in DC."

Her tidbit of news made the thought of the night ahead more tolerable. He'd suspected they'd be meeting her dad and step-mother at one of DC's overpriced, five-star establishments. While Siena wasn't his normal type of restaurant, he knew what to expect there, which meant one less unknown variable tonight. Unfortunately, the biggest one remained—Mark Sherbrooke. The guy had been friendly enough at the wedding, but circum-stances had drastically changed. He might not approve of his only daughter dating a nobody Marine from Rhode Island. From the little Allison told him, her father sounded like the type who'd want the best of everything for his little girl. That included a man from an equally wealthy family.

"Out with it." Allison walked over and took the coffee he'd poured for her. "You're brooding over something. What is it?"

No way am I answering that one. "You need to tell your father what's going on." He transferred the omelet from the pan to a plate and waited. He already knew her answer regarding his statement, but at least it kept her from pestering him about what was really on his mind.

Allison's smile told him she had something up her sleeve. "Tell you what. I'll promise to consider it, if you tell me what's bugging you."

She planned on playing hardball. Her family deserved to know the truth, and he'd promised not to say anything. Getting her to do it was his only option. "Not good enough. I'll share, but *you* need to tell your family."

"You play dirty." She twisted the heart-shaped emerald ring on her finger. He'd noticed she did that to the same ring when-ever she was nervous or deep in thought.

As he watched her do it now, he realized it was the only piece of jewelry she never changed. Since they'd been together, she'd worn other rings as well as countless different bracelets, but the emerald ring always remained on her right hand.

"Okay, I'll tell him."

"Allison—" Rock stopped. "Did you say okay?"

She sighed and frowned. "You're right. But he's not going to take the news well. He and Abby will have to come here before dinner. I can't tell them in a restaurant. Actually, we'll probably never make it to dinner after I tell him."

He guessed she'd made the understatement of the year. And he wouldn't blame the guy if he lost it when he found out the truth.

"Maybe I should invite them back here after dinner instead and tell them then."

As long as she told them tonight, he didn't care when or where she did it. "Up to you."

"Let's do it after. At least then we can enjoy ourselves for a little while." She took a sip of her coffee and then gave him a look. "Your turn. What's going on in that head of yours?"

Damn. "Unsure of what to expect tonight." So he stretched the truth a little. Big friggin' deal. "Last time I had dinner with a girlfriend's parents, I was a junior in high school and it was a Memorial Day cookout."

"You met both Dad and Abby in January."

"We talked for a total of ten minutes at the wedding."

"Don't worry; he's going to love you." She took his hand and gave it a squeeze. "And before I forget, Sara wants to know if I'm bringing a guest to her wedding in June. You talked to her at the fundraiser. Will you come with me? I'm the maid of honor, and I'd like you to meet the rest of the family. Everyone will be there."

Even if he hadn't spoken with Sara at the fundraiser, he'd know which Sherbrooke she referred too. Her cousin Sara was President Sherbrooke's youngest daughter. "I can't."

"Oh," Allison said before he could explain. Releasing his hand, she picked her coffee up again.

"Not because I don't want to. I'm scheduled to leave June fifth and won't be back for six months."

"Six months? Why didn't you say something sooner? The fifth is only a few weeks away."

"I didn't see a point in telling you in the beginning. Then you had more important things to worry about."

"You should've told me." For the first time since he'd met her, she sounded truly upset with him.

From his experience, telling a woman she was right took most of the fight right out of them. It always worked for his dad when he pissed off his mom. "You're right. I should've told you back in March."

"Agreeing with me doesn't get you off the hook." She tried to hide her smile, but the corner of her mouth twitched. "Will you be back for New Years? Every year, the family has a New Year's Eve party in Newport. You could meet everyone—or almost everyone—then."

"Should be." He'd heard about the party from his sister. According to her, it was a Sherbrooke tradition, which went back to the earlier 1900s and everyone from Hollywood movie stars to powerful politicians attended.

"Then consider yourself busy on New Year's Eve."

Sounded like she intended to wait for him. He smiled before he could stop himself.

"What are you smiling about?"

Answering her would give too much away. "Nothing."

Allison opened her mouth to speak, but the doorbell stopped her. "Be right back." The legs of her chair scraped against the tile floor. However, he was out of his chair before she stood up.

"Got it."

"Seriously, it's just Connor. He's got babysitting duty again today."

He didn't care who it was. She wasn't opening the door, end of story. "Probably. I'm still getting it." Rock didn't stick around to hear her argument on the matter.

"Adding doorman to your resume?" Connor asked when he came inside.

Rock ignored his friend. If it meant keeping Allison safe,

he'd add a lot of jobs to his resume. "We're finishing breakfast. Want some coffee?"

"Why not," he answered as they headed for the kitchen. "I owe you one, Raimono, for telling your girlfriend to request me. Got me out of watching over Stan Bonds."

He'd seen Connor on both Monday and Tuesday, but both times Allison had been around too. This was the first time they'd been alone. Rock had expected his buddy to be unhappy with his current assignment, but he didn't seem bothered. "The big mouth oil guy from Texas?"

"He's traveling to Venezuela. Hired the firm again to keep his sorry ass safe. They planned to send me, but the Sherbrooke name pulls higher rank. I'm not complaining. I much prefer working with your girlfriend. She's not what I expected."

He'd thought the same thing back in March. "I know what you mean."

Allison was filling a mug with coffee when they walked in. "Help yourself to anything, Connor, if you're hungry." She handed Connor the mug as she walked by him. "I need to shower. I'll be back."

Rock nodded and glanced down at his watch. What he wouldn't give for an extra thirty minutes or so right now. As it was, he was cutting it close this morning. "I've got to leave in five. See you tonight." He pulled her close before she got farther away. He didn't care if Connor stood in the room. He wasn't letting her leave without a kiss first.

"Have a good day." She dropped a second kiss on his cheek and left.

"Saw the time check," Connor said before he sipped his coffee. "You've got it bad my friend."

Yeah, he did. So what?

~

HAD someone sped up the day or something? One minute, her

computer read ten, and now it said one o'clock. Most of the time, she'd be pleased the end of the workweek was only hours away, and if it didn't mean dinner with her dad and Abby was much closer, she'd be happy this afternoon too. Unfortunately, in a few hours, she had to sit down and tell them everything. Even before this morning, she'd known it was the right thing to do. Some things you couldn't keep from your family, no matter how much you wanted to. A stalker following you around fit into that category. Knowing this fact and telling her dad though were two different things. How did one even start a conversation like that? No matter what her word choice, he'd lose it tonight. She just hoped Rock's presence and the fact she'd not only hired bodyguards but also gotten the police involved would prevent her dad from having a heart attack in her living room.

"Think about something else." Thinking about the task ahead didn't change it or make it go away. It only made her sick to her stomach. Allison focused on her other conversation with Rock this morning, the one they'd had when she'd woken up from her nightmare. *I love you too damn much.* Those had been his words. When she'd asked him out after the Falmouth Foundation fundraiser, she'd only wanted to get to know him better. She hadn't had any expectations past a night out.

Odd how life worked sometimes. In a strange way, she guessed she owed Charles a thank you. If he hadn't shown up at Siena the night she met everyone for dinner, she wouldn't have lied and Rock wouldn't have escorted her to the fundraiser.

Gone for six months. Yuck. Even if neither of them could change the fact, he should've said something before today. She realized when the Marines told him to go, he had no other choice. And it wouldn't have changed her feelings even if she had known sooner, but still, she wished he'd mentioned it sooner. It looked like it was going to be one long summer and fall. She'd need to find something to distract her and make the time go by faster. Maybe a trip somewhere. More than once, Sara had asked her to Alicante in California. Perhaps sometime after Sara and Christopher's honeymoon, she'd visit them for a little while. Her grandparents in New York loved visitors too and often asked her to stay with them. She hadn't visited them in over a year. A week or two up there would kill some time, and she and Nana could get some shopping in. Nana might be in her eighties, but the woman still loved shopping as much as a teenager. As long as she worked while away, Jake wouldn't mind if she took some time off.

Yep, she'd find ways to make the months pass. And until Rock left, she'd enjoy their time together as much as possible, considering the circumstances. So far, the police had no leads. The only fingerprints they'd found in her house had belonged to either her or Rock. When they informed her of their findings, she'd almost cried. She'd been positive they'd find something. Even if they hadn't been able to match the print to anyone yet, at least it would've been some hard physical evidence. Right now, they had none. If she didn't know better, she'd think she'd imagined it all. Too many things pointed at someone being after her, including the bullet through Rock's apartment window.

Technically, the police had nothing to tie the shooting with someone breaking into her house, but she knew they were related. Rock agreed, although he'd admitted he didn't know if the bullet had been intended to hurt her or scare her. Either way, she didn't care. She just wanted the madman caught and her life normal again. She loved having Rock with her every night. Both Connor and Neil were nice guys, but she hated having a shadow everywhere she went.

Allison's mood plummeted straight to her Prada pumps. *Positive thoughts, think positive thoughts. Only about a month until my niece or nephew is born.* If thoughts of a baby weren't a positive thing, she didn't know what was. She couldn't wait to meet Trent and Addie's son or daughter and then spoil him or her like a good aunt. *Sara's wedding.* Even if Rock wouldn't be around then, she couldn't wait for the wedding. Although not her only female cousin, she'd always been closest to Sara. Her cousin had dated her fair share of jerks before her relationship with Christopher, Jake's best friend, and Allison had never seen her happier.

Slowly, her mood inched its way up from her toes. Now if she could just get the sick knot out of her stomach, the day wouldn't be a total loss.

~

ALLISON STEPPED off the elevator a few hours later and walked toward the reception desk. She'd needed a little afternoon pick-me-up, and the best place around for a coffee was the Coffee Factory Café next door.

"Miss Sherbrooke, you have a visitor," Denise said from behind the reception desk. "He arrived not long after you left."

Before Allison managed a word, Connor stepped closer, the fingers on his right hand flexing. "Did he give you a name?"

More than ever, she appreciated Connor's presence. She didn't have any meetings scheduled today, so who waited for her?

"He said his name was Hunter Perkins," Denise replied, reaching for the phone. "Should I call building security?

Hunter? Here? While odd, it didn't require a call into building security. "Don't worry about it, Denise. I know Hunter."

"A friend?" Connor asked, his posture telling her he still didn't like the idea of someone showing up unexpectedly.

"More like an acquaintance. I used to date his older brother, Charles. I've known him a while." She walked toward the office waiting area.

When Hunter spotted her, he stood and stepped forward. The movement only caused Connor to move so he walked a step or two in front of her. "Connor, really, it's okay. I know him." She kept her voice low so neither Denise nor Hunter heard her comment. Her constant shadow remained where he stood directly between her and Hunter.

He made as if he intended to embrace her when she got closer, but then his arms fell by his sides. "Allison, I hope I'm not disrupting anything. I was in the area and wanted to say hi," Hunter said with a smile.

"Nah, we just stepped out for coffee. Come on in my office." She'd seen Hunter numerous times when she'd visited Charles and his family. She'd always found him a little odd, although she couldn't explain why. That didn't mean she had to be rude and ask him to leave. Besides, a visit with him provided a nice little distraction from her earlier thoughts.

Connor's tightlipped expression let her know his thoughts on the situation, but he didn't argue. Instead, he followed them back toward her office and to his seat outside the door.

"What are you doing in Alexandria?" Allison asked once they both sat.

"Interviewed for a summer internship at Novo and Sullivan. I have another with Griffin, White, and Crosby next week."

She'd heard of the well-known law firm located a few blocks over. With one of her questions answered, she posed her other one. "How did you know I worked here?"

"Charles mentioned it when we talked. He said he saw you with Trent and your sister-in-law."

Duh. Charles, she should have thought of him. Hunter and Charles talked a lot, or at least they had when they'd been together. "They were down for a fundraiser." With her questions answered, she searched for some conversation starters. School came to mind first. Hunter attended Georgetown University. "How's the semester going?"

"It's a breeze. Wish the fall semester had been as easy."

"Football must take up a lot of your time in the fall." She didn't recall what position he played, but she remembered Charles telling her his brother played for the Hoyas.

"Yeah, and I tore my ACL last season," Hunter answered,

then went into way more detail than she needed about the play that caused the injury and the rehab afterward.

Twenty minutes later, Connor knocked on the door, saving her from any further football plays. "Miss Sherbrooke, you asked me to remind you when it was four."

"Thanks, Connor," she said, playing along. Honestly, she'd had enough football talk for one day, but Hunter hadn't given her a chance to interrupt him. "I've got this bad habit of losing track of time and I'm meeting my dad and stepmom for dinner tonight."

"Gotcha. Saw your dad when I visited Providence last month." He stood but didn't make a move to the door. "If I get the internship at Novo and Sullivan, I'll need a place in Alexandria. Any areas you recommend?"

"I'm over on Cameron Street. Everything around there is nice."

Hunter nodded and smiled. "Thanks. I'll check it out. Talk to you later."

She waited until her guest left before she went for the door herself and opened it. "How did you know I needed a break?"

Connor lowered the coffee he still nursed and looked at her. "Just wanted him out of your office. Didn't like the guy."

"He's harmless. But thanks anyway. I thought I'd hear about every play from last season."

"Not a football fan?"

"How'd you guess?" Although perhaps if it had been someone else giving her the season recap, she wouldn't have minded so much. Rock could give her a lesson on the proper way to wash dishes in his sexy voice and she'd enjoy it. "I'm not going to get anything else done today. As soon as I close out my computer programs, we can go."

"Ready when you are, Miss Sherbrooke."

∾

Rock thanked Detective Graves, the officer who was investigating the shooting at his apartment, and ended the call. While the police had found fingerprints on the casing recovered in the parking lot, it had not matched any on record. The only positive news from the call, if you could call it positive, had been that they'd matched the bullet to a weapon used in a fatal robbery the previous year. However, the homicide remained unsolved and the official from Dumfries didn't know how the weapon had made its way back into circulation. At the time of the robbery, the gun had been found in the dumpster outside the convenience store and taken into police evidence. Graves claimed all this was further evidence the shooting at his apartment had been a random gang related act and nothing else.

He didn't buy it. He tried convincing the guy otherwise. Although the detective had remained polite, he'd more or less told Rock he had no clue. He recognized a hopeless case. If the detective didn't want to hear it, he wouldn't waste his breath. The cops in Alexandria knew about the shooting. They might have better luck getting Graves and the Dumfries's police force onboard. Either way, it didn't change his mission. Until he left next month, he'd do everything possible to keep Allison safe.

After passing through the base exit, he headed for Interstate 95. Typically, he took the interstate straight to US-1. Since tonight of all nights he couldn't be late, he'd checked traffic reports before leaving. According to them, an accident had traffic on US-1 backed up for miles, which meant if he hoped to reach Allison's with enough time, he'd have to take an alternate route.

Rock's smartphone beeped while he waited at the traffic light and he glanced at it.

Addie's water broke. They're on their way to hospital. I'll call when I have more news. Your dad and I are on our way over there, the message from his mom said.

He reread the message. He'd hoped she'd go into labor early and have the baby before he left in June. Now maybe he'd get to meet his nephew before he came back in the winter. Both he and Allison were convinced the baby was a boy. His sister and Trent kept denying they knew, but on more than one occasion, Addie referred to the baby as "him." Allison was so positive in fact she'd ordered dozens of baby boy outfits, which she'd showed him the moment they arrived. He'd been blown away by the tiny size of them. The idea another human could fit into them boggled the mind.

Before he did anything more than hit reply, his phone rang.

"Trent's taking Addie to the hospital. She's in labor," Allison said before he managed any kind of greeting. "Dad just called me."

"Got a text from my mom. Are we canceling dinner tonight?" He understood if Mark Sherbrooke wanted to head back up to Providence. A guy's first grandbaby wasn't born everyday.

"If I didn't know better, I'd say you're afraid of seeing my dad."

Afraid? Hell no. A bit reluctant perhaps. "Figured he'd want to be there for your brother."

"He does, but he also wants to have dinner with us since he's already in the area. We're meeting them at the Washington Grille instead. It's closer to the airport. Right after dinner, they'll head back to Providence. He's already told his flight crew about the changes."

Sounded like they had it all figured out.

"He invited us to fly back with them."

Stuck on a plane with her dad and stepmom wasn't how he pictured his Friday night.

"Don't worry. I declined the offer," Allison continued on before he said a word. "I didn't think you'd want to travel with them, so I told Dad you couldn't leave the area this weekend."

Already, he regretted the words he intended to say. "If you want to fly back with him, we can." Her stalker was in Virginia, not Providence. By the time he figured out she'd left, she'd be in

Rhode Island. Assuming they stayed at her father's estate, which he guessed had a top-notch security system, he could protect her just as well in Providence as he could here.

"I love you," Allison said.

She'd told him the same thing early today, but it still sounded surreal.

"I already told him we can't fly up tonight. How about we plan on going up next weekend?"

As long as she was willing to wait, he'd go next weekend or any other time she wanted. "You got it. See ya soon. Love ya."

CHAPTER 17

How? How had he made such a stupid mistake and not locked the deadbolt on the back door? He'd been so careful each and every time he'd gone inside. And it had always been so easy. Only the very first time had it been tricky.

It was Raimono's fault he'd made an error. If the jerk hadn't touched Allison, he would've remained calm and not slipped up. Now, not only did she have Raimono living with her and bodyguards in tow, but the police were involved too. If not for Kitty at the station, he wouldn't know the reason behind the police visit to Allison's house earlier in the week. Her knowledge had kept him from visiting Allison's house again. The first thing the police would've told her when they came out was to change her alarm code, which meant he'd have no way of turning it off. He didn't need half the Alexandria police department arriving after him. Assuming he was able to get in at all with his key. He suspected the police would've suggested she get her door locks changed too. It didn't matter now anyway.

Their little precautions only meant his plans required adjusting. He'd made all the changes without any difficulty. Having a friend who could hack into any computer or security system came in handy. Too bad he'd have to die too. Who knew when he'd have need for such talent again? Unfortunately, if he let Roger live, there'd always be one person out there who knew the truth. Right now, Roger agreed to keep his mouth shut and take the money they'd agreed on. What if he changed his mind and demanded more money? Or even worse, went to the cops? No, he couldn't risk it no matter how valuable Roger may be in the future. When Roger came back to collect his money, he wouldn't leave.

Yes, tonight, everything would occur as planned. This time tomorrow, Rocco Raimono would be dead, his body burned past recognition along with Roger's. Even better, he and Allison would be at his house in Maine where no one would find them.

Just a few more hours. He watched her walk inside with her bodyguard and then he turned away from the windows. Too bad he'd been forced to change his original plan. He liked this house. It had a lot of character to it. History too, if what the real estate agent told him when he bought the place was true. Maybe when he came back from Maine he'd see if he could find a house similar to this one. He liked the area and planned on staying in Alexandria for the foreseeable future. *I wish you could've lived, my love. If only you'd waited for me.*

CHAPTER 18

MARK SHERBROOKE'S face lit up and he enveloped Allison in a hug. Before letting her go, he kissed her cheek. "I've missed you. You need to come home and visit us."

"Miss you too, Dad, but I've been busy." She moved toward her stepmother, leaving Rock inside her father's crosshairs—not the place he wanted to be.

"Rock, it's nice to see you again. How have you been?" Mark extended his hand, a welcoming smile still on his face.

"Fine, sir. And you?" Rock returned Mark's surprisingly firm handshake.

"Well, but please call me Mark. None of that 'sir' business," he answered.

Calling her father by his first name would take some serious getting used to. His parents had installed the belief that you never address your elders by their first name. The Corps had only further drilled respect into him. "I'll try to remember."

"Don't worry; I'll remind you if you forget," Allison supplied, sitting down at the table.

"That's my girl." Mark's comment sounded similar to something his dad would say, and it somehow made the guy seem more approachable.

"Have you talked to Trent again?" Allison asked.

Other than the text message he'd received from his mom, he hadn't gotten any more information about Addie's condition. He considered trying his sister's phone, but figured it would be pointless. If she was still in labor, the last thing she'd want was a conversation. And if the baby had been born, she'd want to be holding the baby not her phone.

Mark's smile faded. "He hasn't called again."

"Be honest," his wife added as she patted his hand.

Mark cleared his throat at his wife's comment and then spoke again. "I called him before we came here."

"He couldn't resist. You know how impatient he can be," Abby said.

Rock knew the woman wasn't Allison's biological mother, but judging by the interaction between them, the two women shared similar personality traits.

"Dad impatient? No way." Allison tried to maintain a shocked expression. "He's the most patient man I know," she said as she lost the battle and her expression changed to one of pure amusement.

"I wanted to make sure they'd gotten settled in at the hospital."

"Understandable, don't you agree, Allison?" Abby asked, her lips twitching. The woman enjoyed giving her husband a hard time. Judging by the way Mark went along with it, he didn't mind.

"Completely. Did Trent give you an update?"

"He said they'd been admitted and that Sal and Marta were there with them."

Good. Addie would want their parents close.

"I'm anxious to get there myself tonight. There's nothing like meeting your child, or in this case, grandchild for the first time." Mark's voice grew thick with emotion. "I was right by your mom's side when all of you were born, although I almost didn't make it in time for Gray. He couldn't wait to get into this world. Hopefully, Addie will have a similar delivery to Gray's tonight. But enough talk about Addie and Trent. Tell me about things here."

Allison gave him a sideways glance. If they'd been in a private setting, he would've encouraged her to get it over with and tell her dad about the current problem. With so many people around them and considering the response she predicted from her dad, Rock kept his mouth closed.

"Jake's a slave driver," Allison said. "Do you know he took two weeks off when Garret was born and left me all his work?"

Rock sat back and listened to the conversation between Allison and her family. Although it was only one meeting, it appeared as though she had a strong relationship with both her dad and stepmom. A few of his buddies in high school had step-parents and, with one exception, all their relationships had been cold. In those cases though, the parents had divorced before remarrying. He didn't have the details about the how, but he knew Allison's mom passed away several years ago. He guessed his sister knew what happened. It seemed like something a man would share with his wife. He'd stopped himself from asking his sister despite his curiosity. He'd dislike someone poking around in his personal life, especially about something like the death of a parent. Besides, he figured enough people poked into her business because of her last name. He didn't need to do it too. When she wanted to tell him, she would.

"It's too bad you cannot get away this weekend. I'm sure Addie and your parents would love to see you. Marta mentioned you don't make it home much," Abby said once Allison had finished filling her dad in all about her work at the Falmouth Foundation.

Abigail Sherbrooke and his mother discussed him? He couldn't picture such a conversation. "Not too often. She gets it though."

"Understanding and liking it are two very different things. It's only been a few months and I miss my regular lunch dates with Allison. I can't imagine going a year or more without seeing her and the boys."

Sounded like not only Allison but also her four brothers had a close relationship with their stepmother.

"We'll be up next weekend. Maybe we can have lunch then and ask Addie along too. We'll leave the men in charge of the baby. By then, Trent will have had a whole week to master changing a diaper." For about the third time since they'd sat down, Allison checked her phone for any text messages. He'd noticed her dad doing the same thing.

Rock moved his hand toward his own pocket, but stopped when the hair on his neck decided to march toward his scalp. Someone watched them.

He made a visual pass around the restaurant. Not a single person stood out as not belonging. If Allison's stalker sat inside, he blended in with the well-dressed individuals. Did that mean her stalker was an older individual? Except for him and Allison, everyone looked to be at least in their fifties. He'd expected the SOB to be younger.

"Abby, is that William and Louisa near the windows?" Mark asked, interrupting his wife as she and Allison further discussed a possible lunch date next weekend.

Allison's stepmom looked toward the windows. He did the same and found the couple in question staring back at their table. *Explains whose watching us.*

"It is." She sent the couple a wave, which brought them to their feet and toward the table.

"Louisa and Abby used to serve on Barrington's Historical Preservation Society together before her husband got elected to Congress," Allison explained as he watched the couple cross the room and the sense of being watched disappeared.

Even with the minor mystery solved, he examined the room one more time. Everyone looked harmless enough. That didn't mean they were. The sooner he got Allison home behind a locked door, the better.

~

"Ouch, that looks bad," Allison said when she stepped out of his truck, her eyes fixed on the accident down the street.

He agreed. Judging by the damage to both the vehicle and the utility pole, he doubted the driver or any passengers had survived the accident. "Probably some idiot drank too much and got behind the wheel." He'd almost lost a friend in a drunk driving accident. Somehow though, the guy managed to make it through. Unfortunately, he now spent his days confined to a wheelchair. "Hope he didn't have anyone with him." Rock touched her back and gave her a little nudge. Outside, she remained too exposed.

Allison took the hint and started walking. "Dad really likes you." Her hair brushed against his arm while he unlocked the front door. "Abby does too. They're looking forward to our visit next weekend."

Rock pushed open the door and stepped inside first. The chance of someone waiting inside was slim, but better safe than sorry. "How'd you come to that conclusion?" Allison had left him only once all night when she and Abby went to the restroom, so he'd heard everything her father said.

"Abby told me in the ladies' room. And Dad whispered it when he hugged me before we left." Allison flipped the switch near the door, but nothing happened. Considering the accident outside, he expected no power.

"Tell me you've got flashlights."

Just enough light came through the windows for him to see her expression, but the sunlight was fading fast. "Afraid of the dark? Don't worry, I'll protect you tonight." She kissed his cheek before she passed by him.

"The backup battery for the security system is only going to last a few hours. Assuming we can arm it at all. Some won't let you set them if only battery power is available. It's a stupid design, in my opinion. Either way, it's getting dark, and if the powers not back soon, it'll leave us vulnerable. We'll need some light." He had one flashlight, but he'd prefer more. "If we can arm the system, do ya know the battery life?"

Her smile vanished. "Right. Sorry. I didn't even think of the alarm."

He hated she needed to now. Until they got the bastard, they had no alternative.

"Uh, no. I've got no idea how long the battery will last. The system was here when I moved in, so I don't know anything about it. But I've got flashlights and candles. If you want to let Baxter out, I'll get them."

Baxter's whine got louder the longer they spoke. Once the dog heard voices in the house, he assumed it meant he needed out of his crate so he could play or eat. He didn't seem to care which came first. "Grab any extra batteries you have for the flashlights too."

Since he'd moved in, they'd kept Baxter's crate in the laundry room off the kitchen. The dog hated it, and Rock didn't blame him. Most of the time he left Baxter free in his apartment. Only on those rare occasions did he lock him up for long periods of time. Even when he got deployed and the dog stayed with his parents, Baxter remained free to roam the house while they worked. Allison's place was a different story.

"How ya doing, buddy?" He crouched down and unlocked the door. Right away, the dog bolted outside into the hall, turned around, and raced back to him. Baxter stopped long enough to lick Rock's hand before he bolted out the door again and toward the kitchen. He'd learned quickly to head for the back door when he wanted outside.

"Didn't find too many extra batteries. But we've got two big Maglites and this." She held up the headlamp designed for running outside.

Rock let the dog out into the backyard, if you could even call it a yard. It was more like a fenced in square patch of grass barely large enough for the small patio table and chairs placed out there. However, it gave Baxter a place to take care of his business, so Rock didn't have to leave Allison alone while he walked him.

"And I've got one upstairs." He always kept at least one compact-sized, lithium-powered flashlight around. The things were powerful despite their size. He'd even bought his mother one for Christmas a year or two ago to keep in her purse.

A scratching at the back door let them know Baxter wanted back inside, and Allison dropped everything on the table. "I got it."

Rock moved before she finished her sentence. "Don't think so."

"People don't scratch at doors, Rock. It's the dog ready to come in." Her voice projected annoyance and frustration.

Neither changed his mind. "It sucks, I know. But for now, I'll do whatever it takes to keep *you* safe." He let Baxter inside, and the dog went straight for the cupboard where they'd stashed his food and treats.

"He knows what he wants." Allison grabbed the dog's dish from the floor and filled it with food.

Before she moved away, Rock stepped behind her and grabbed her around the waist. "He's not the only one." He pushed her hair away from her neck and kissed the skin just below her ear.

"I once read husbands and wives take on each others personality traits after being together for a long time. I guess it applies to men and their dogs too. Just promise you won't start howling to get my attention like Baxter."

He kissed the same spot again before he slipped a hand under her blouse. "There are better ways of getting your attention." Her stomach muscles contracted as he ran his finger across her skin and up toward her bra. When his hand covered her breast, her head fell back against his shoulder.

"What do ya think? Do I have your attention?"

"Mission accomplished."

"Good." He'd discovered weeks ago how much she enjoyed it when he teased her nipples. He dipped his fingers into her bra, intent on touching them now. Baxter's jump into the air stopped him as the dog's head bumped into the bowl, sending pieces of food everywhere.

"Another personality trait you both share, impatience."

With the moment ruined, he moved his hand and grabbed the now half full dog bowl. "Thanks a lot, buddy. I owe you one," he said to the dog, who at the moment was too busy inhaling the food scattered around the floor to even look in his direction.

"At least he's cleaning up the mess."

Rock gave the dog a dirty look before moving and putting the dish down. "How thoughtful of him." The tap the metal dish made when it hit the floor caught Baxter's attention, and he looked up then trotted over to it. "Let's see if the alarm system will activate."

Allison beat him to the control panel near the back door. When she punched in her code and it beeped, she threw him a thumbs-up, closed the panel, and sauntered back over to him. "Nice and safe for the night." Her fingertips skimmed up his torso. With slow movements, she unknotted his tie and pulled it off. "I think we should go upstairs and find a way to amuse ourselves."

He watched her undo each shirt button. When she finished, she pushed the fabric away and kissed his chest. The heat from her lips seeped though his undershirt, branding his skin. "Unless you have a better idea?"

Better idea? He had one.

Picking her up, Rock sat her on the edge of the barstool near the counter, shoving her skirt higher in the process. Going down to his knees, he kissed her knee and worked his way up her inner thigh. When he reached his destination, he pushed her damp panties aside but didn't touch her. Instead, he stared, drinking in the sight before him, committing it to memory for those months ahead when half a world separated them.

On the stool, Allison wiggled closer to the edge. She grabbed his hand, and he allowed her to guide it. He touched the slick, wet skin and his penis pressed against the front of his pants, demanding to join the fun. "Damn, you're so ready." He let one finger dip inside.

In response, Allison closed her eyes as her head fell back and she moaned.

Damn, he wanted her. First, he'd make her come with his mouth. He'd fantasized about pleasuring her like that for a long time. Afterward, he'd take her upstairs and bury himself in her and make her come again.

Rock moved his finger back and forth, enjoying the feel of her muscles contracting around him. Before he lost all control, he stopped.

On the stool, Allison moved and opened her eyes. "What's wrong?" she panted, her chest rising and falling quickly.

Not a damn thing. Rather than answer, he replaced his finger with his tongue.

～

WARM LIPS BRUSHED against her forehead. The memory of where those oh-so talented lips had been earlier tonight rushed forward, setting her face on fire. She'd never been on the receiving end of oral sex. Her ex had loved when she pleasured him that way. In fact, he'd encouraged it so much she'd gotten the impression he preferred oral sex. Despite all the times she'd fulfilled his desires, he'd never reciprocated. Until tonight, she'd not known what she was missing.

"You're quiet." Rock's voice rumbled in her ear, distracting her from her current thoughts. "Something wrong?"

"Nope. Just thinking." Wrong? If she could freeze time, she would. Right now, everything felt perfect.

"About?" He played with her hair. Before they went out,

she'd tied it back in a twist, but Rock had pulled out all the pins holding it up.

Her face burned hotter at the mere thought of admitting she'd been thinking about what transpired in the kitchen and hoping he'd do it again. They'd both enjoyed themselves. *There's no reason to be embarrassed.* "Earlier, in the kitchen." Allison considered the temporary blackout a plus. She suspected her face resembled a bright red raspberry.

Rock leaned over her, his face mere inches away from hers. "Me too," he whispered the words, and she caught the briefest scent of cherries. The man loved to suck on those hard cherry candies. She noticed he kept a whole bag stashed in his truck and he'd added several bags to the kitchen pantry.

Despite the darkness, she closed her eyes in anticipation of his kiss. She sensed his movements as he came closer. Ready for him, she parted her lips.

He stopped, his whole body tense under her hands. "Did you hear something?" His voice remained low, and the humor she'd heard in it disappeared.

She shook her head before remembering he couldn't see her in the dark. "No. Maybe it's the trucks down the street." The last time she'd looked outside, two utility trucks and a police cruiser remained working on the downed pole. Since the power hadn't returned, she assumed they still worked out there.

"I don't think so. It sounded like it came from inside." The mattress shifted as he moved away from her. "Stay here. I'm going to check the house. Lock the bedroom door behind me."

Allison grabbed the flashlight from the nightstand. Pointing it down so she didn't blind Rock with the bright light, she switched it on. "If someone broke in, the alarm would've gone off. Baxter probably needed some water or there's another mouse in the attic. I had one in February right after I moved in." When they'd gone downstairs for a bottle of wine, they'd checked the user manual. According to it, the battery in the system would last for twelve hours. The power hadn't been out that long.

"Stay here, Ally." He yanked on some jeans and an undershirt then grabbed the pistol on the nightstand. "And lock the door."

CHAPTER 19

FINALLY. He put the lock picking set back into his pocket. He'd hoped the key would work, but he'd known it was a long shot. The new locks installed were a definite upgrade. They'd managed to slow him down but not stop him. Nothing could stop him. He was smarter than all of them.

He pushed the door open and entered the pitch-black kitchen. Before moving any farther, he switched on the recon LED flashlight he'd purchased. He'd tested it out at home, and it performed as promised. It provided him with light and preserved his night vision. Not that he needed much light. He'd visited the house enough. The back stairway up to the second floor was on his right. By using it, he avoided walking past the laundry room. On his last visit, he'd spotted a dog bed near the pet crate. He assumed it meant at night the dog slept in there. The last thing he wanted was to alert the dog. From his past visits, he knew as long as the dog didn't see him, he remained quiet.

Taking a step up, he paused and savored the giddiness making his heart pump faster. His skin itched for the feel of Allison against him. His ears longed for her screams when he punished her for choosing Raimono instead of him.

He pushed away the tantalizing vision. *Go time.*

CHAPTER 20

SHE PACED from the bed to the windows. On her second pass, she stopped and peeked outside. Both utility trucks remained parked down the street, along with a police cruiser. *Power's probably still out. Darn.* Allison let the curtain fall and tried the lamp closest to her anyway. Nothing. She hoped she was right and whatever sound Rock heard had been the workers outside. She didn't want any more mice in the attic or anywhere else in the house.

The doorknob rattled and Allison moved to open it. *He told me to lock it. Why would he try opening it?* The thought brought her to a standstill. Rock would call out and ask her to open the door. He wouldn't forget his instructions to lock it and try opening the door.

Allison stepped back until her legs hit the bed's footboard. She swept her flashlight around the room and looked for anything she could use for a weapon. The door lock would only slow a person down, not stop them. It wasn't that kind of lock. She needed some kind of weapon until Rock got to her.

Rock. Oh, God. If the intruder made it to the bedroom door, did that mean Rock was hurt? Was he dead downstairs? A hand gripped her heart and squeezed as a scream fought its way up her throat. *Don't make a sound. Rock's fine. He'll be here.*

She searched around again for a weapon. Rock had taken his pistol with him. She didn't see the knife he often had clipped to his belt. *Hide in the closet.* Again, not a solution, but just a way to buy Rock some time.

Pop. The simple lock in the doorknob released. In silence, the door swung open. A large male form filled the doorway.

She prepared to scream. Then she got a look at the intruder's face. Her voice failed her as her mind swirled with questions.

"Hunter?" No, it couldn't be. She was dreaming. This was some terrible nightmare again. Why would Hunter Perkins be breaking into her bedroom? They were, well, maybe not friends, but at least friendly acquaintances. They'd talked this afternoon in her office. He'd asked for recommendations for places to live in the city. He couldn't be standing in her doorway.

She made eye contact with him before he looked toward the bed behind her. When he glanced back, she saw the surprise reflected in his eyes. She saw something else too. Coldness like she'd never seen in anyone. *He expected me to be asleep in bed.*

Fear gripped her. Her knees shook. She looked away from his face. Her flashlight reflected light off the large blade in his right hand and she glimpsed the pistol on his hip. *He's going to kill me.*

"Allison." The same voice she'd heard in her office whispered her name, and Hunter's lips curled into a wicked smile. "My sweet Allison."

Ice enveloped her body and she trembled.

ROCK CLEARED THE LIBRARY. He'd checked almost all rooms on the first floor and nothing. Maybe there was a mouse in the attic. Old homes were notorious for critters getting in. He closed the door behind him. Regardless, he'd check the kitchen and laundry room while down here.

Creak. The noise stopped him dead, and he listened. *Creak.* No mouse made sounds like that.

Rock bolted into kitchen and up the backstairs, his bare feet silent on the thick runner. A tall, athletically built figure stepped into Allison's bedroom. Red filled his vision and he raised his pistol. One shot through the back and the SOB would be down.

He lined up the sights and went for the trigger. *Stop.* Enough rage cleared his mind and his dad's words echoed in his head. *Know what's on the other side of what you're shooting.* He couldn't see Allison. He didn't know where in the room she stood. What if the bullet went through the bastard and into her? No, he couldn't fire until he knew he had a clean shot.

"Hunter?" Allison's voice reached him down the hall. She told him about her unexpected visit from Hunter Perkins at the office.

Moving his finger from the trigger, he considered his next move. So far, the jerk didn't know he was mere feet away.

"Allison," Hunter's voice barely reached Rock. "My sweet Allison. It's time."

Everything around him stopped. He charged down the hall, prepared to tackle the jerk to the floor and put a bullet between his damn eyes.

Hunter turned and raised his knife. He'd lost the element of surprise, but it didn't matter. Only protecting Allison did.

Rock moved and Hunter's blade made contact with air.

He caught sight of Allison directly behind the SOB. He couldn't fire now. Not with her so close.

Before he could swipe at him again, he grabbed Hunter's forearm and dug his fingers into the pressure points. He'd sent men to their knees with this move. Hunter's blade hit the hard wood floor, but he remained upright.

Pain radiated through Rock's cheek and blood filled his mouth.

HE DROPPED THE KNIFE. She heard it hit the floor and shined the flashlight toward the men. She'd never seen anything like it. Both men were about the same size, and it was obvious they'd both learned some hand-to-hand fighting techniques. While Rock appeared the more skilled of the two, Hunter looked to be holding his own.

Suddenly, Hunter got the upper hand and smashed Rock's head into the wall. Somehow, she needed to help. She passed the light across the floor in search of Hunter's knife. Once again, the light bounced off the lethal-looking blade. Should she try for it? All Hunter had to do was move a little and he'd be able to pick it up again and stab Rock. Maybe she could get to it first.

Near the wall, one of the men grunted before a deafening bang exploded in the room. Her ears rang with pain, but she didn't stop to consider why. Instead, she dove for the knife. A heavy foot came down on her hand just as her fingers touched handle. Allison cried out as Hunter grabbed her around the waist and pulled her against him.

"You're mine. You moved here to be closer to me." Hunter's arm tightened around her waist, making it hard to breathe. "It's your fault, Allison. He has to die tonight because of you. How could you let that piece of trash touch you?" He jabbed something hard into her side. "Only I have the right to touch you."

Muted light suddenly filled the room as electricity flowed through the lamp she'd tried switching on earlier. She wished the power had stayed out.

Rock faced them. He had his pistol drawn and pointed at Hunter. Already his right eye had turned an ugly purple and blood trickled down his face. It was nothing compared to the blood soaking his undershirt.

She gagged at the sight and her head swam. *Keep it together.* She couldn't pass out now.

"Drop the gun." Hunter pressed the pistol farther into her side, and she bit down on her tongue rather than cry out.

How was this possible? She'd always thought Hunter a little odd, but not batshit crazy. Whatever hold the man had on reality had completely left him. He planned on killing Rock and it was her fault.

"If you don't, it'll be your fault when the princess starts suffering." Hunter kissed her temple. "Don't worry. We'll still have our fun together, Allison. Nothing will get in the way of what I have planned."

The wine she'd drank rushed up into her mouth and she swallowed it back down.

Slowly, Rock lowered his gun.

"I said drop it."

Rock's eyes never strayed from Hunter's face when he spoke. "Move yours away from her." His voice remained calm and authoritative. She couldn't detect a hint of fear. Nice to know at least one of them wasn't ready to pee their pants before passing out.

"You're not in control here." Despite his reply, he pulled the gun away a little. "I am."

"Kill me. Leave her alone. I forced her. She wanted to be with you. I wouldn't let her." Rock took a step forward as he spoke. "She begged me to let her find you. Get rid of me and you can have her."

"I knew it." He kissed her temple again, the slight touch making her skin crawl. "But she still needs to pay too." The arm around her waist loosened enough for her to breathe. "Stop moving!" Hunter shouted when Rock took another step forward. "Put the gun on the floor and kick it away or she starts paying right now while you watch."

It looked like his mouth had stopped bleeding, but the spot on Rock's shirt continued to get bigger. He was going to die and it was because of her. There had to be something she could do. "Hunter, please—"

"Shut up." He squeezed her again. "This is between him and me. I'll take care of *you* later."

No. She watched in stunned horror as Rock followed Hunter's orders and put the pistol on the floor.

"Last chance. Kick it over here."

Don't do it. Don't do it.

He gave the weapon a nudge with his toe and it skidded toward them, leaving Rock defenseless.

Everything after that happened in a blur. One minute, Hunter had his gun pressed into her side, and the next, he'd raised it. On instinct, she pushed Hunter's arm so the gun no longer pointed straight at Rock's chest. Another deafening shot split the silence in the room and then suddenly Hunter pitched backward, his arm around her loosening enough so she could roll away.

Both men struggled on the floor. A third shot rang out and bits of plaster from the ceiling rained down. She raced for Rock's gun. They'd never made it out to the range, but she could do this. She had to do this. Rock's life depended on it.

Shaking hands and damp palms were not a good combination when trying to get a proper grip. She mouthed a little prayer and tried to remember everything Rock had told her about aiming. She only wanted to hit Hunter. She'd never forgive herself if she shot Rock instead.

It looked like something out of a movie. One minute, the men were grappling on the floor, and the next, Rock plunged a knife into Hunter's neck. Blood spurted from the wound and Allison dropped to her knees, her eyes closed. Her head swam as if she'd spent an entire afternoon on a spinning ride at an amusement park.

"Ally." Rock sounded in pain.

She opened her eyes. Both Rock and Hunter lay on the floor. Blood covered Hunter's neck and puddled under him. His eyes remained open, but she couldn't tell if he was alive or not. She didn't care either.

Allison stepped around Hunter and kneeled down. "I need

to call for help." Although Rock remained breathing, he looked in rough shape. His white undershirt looked like someone had tried tie-dying it red, and she could see the bullet hole in it. His left thigh was also drenched in blood. Her phone should be near the bed. "I'll be right back." She kissed his forehead.

Rock took her hand before she stood. "You okay?" he grunted.

She couldn't even imagine the pain he was in. "I'm fine." Physically anyway. She'd deal with the mental ramifications later. Right now, getting him help was all that mattered. "You need help. I'm just going to grab my phone." Despite his injuries, Rock gripped her hand as if he never intended on letting go. "I'll be right back. Promise." She pulled away and he grimaced.

"Love ya." The deep sexy voice she'd enjoyed listening to contained only pain when he spoke, which was something she never wanted to hear in his voice again.

"I love you too." Hot tears burned her eyes, blurring her vision. *Cry later.* She sprinted for her smartphone. She dialed 911 and walked back to Rock's side and took his hand. He'd closed his eyes, but his chest rose and fell. *He's going to be okay.*

"911, what's your location?" the dispatcher asked.

"45 Cameron Street, Alexandria. I need the police and two ambulances. My boyfriend was shot and someone else stabbed." If Hunter was alive, he'd need help too.

"Are the victims responsive?" the dispatcher asked, her voice calm and cool considering the information she collected.

She gave Rock's hand a squeeze. For a moment, he opened his eyes and looked at her. "One is." *At least for now*, she thought but didn't repeat. "I'm not sure about the other."

"The police and paramedics are on their way. I'm going to stay on the line with you until they arrive."

Please get here fast. Until they did, she needed to do something. Try to help in some way, because every second that ticked by, more blood flowed from his wounds. She'd gotten her first aid certification. She could help him.

"Are you willing to administer first aid until they get there?"

"Yes."

"Okay, here is what I need you to do. Grab some towels or cloth," the dispatcher said before she rattled off more instructions.

Allison listened as she grabbed T-shirts from her drawers so she could apply pressure. *I can do this.* Rock had saved her life. Now she had to help save his.

CHAPTER 21

THE DOOR OPENED, but she didn't turn around. What if it was the doctor coming in to tell her Rock hadn't made it? When the paramedics took him out of the house, he'd matched the sheet on the stretcher. Not to mention all the blood. The bedroom floor had been covered with it. She kept reminding herself it hadn't all been Rock's. Some belonged to Hunter.

Hunter. He was her stalker. She still couldn't process the truth. He'd seemed normal, like any other college-aged man. In many ways, he'd been like his older brother, Charles. How had he gone off the deep end like that? She rubbed her temple and pushed away the image of him lying there, his eyes staring at the ceiling and his shirt soaked. When the two sets of paramedics arrived, one descended on Rock and got to work. She overheard the second team say Hunter was gone before a police officer managed to escort her from the room. She didn't see what the paramedics did after she went downstairs.

The same police officer later drove her to the hospital, where she'd been shown to a private waiting area with hospital security officers posted in the hall so nosy reporters left her alone. That had been a while ago.

"Allison?" The door clicked closed and her cousin called out to her.

Turning around, she rushed toward Jake and flung her arms around him. When the hospital suggested she call someone to stay with her, she'd immediately contacted him. When he didn't answer, she'd left a message sharing bits and pieces of what happened and hoped he checked it soon. He'd called a short time later and promised to be right there.

For a few minutes, neither spoke as the tears she'd held back so far exploded. Jake rubbed her back as she sobbed, her entire body shaking. Even when the tears subsided, she clung to him, her anchor in the crazy night.

"Are you sure you're okay? He didn't hurt you?" Jake asked, unable to hide the worry in his voice.

She sniffed several times as she nodded her forehead, rubbing against his shirt. "I'm... I'm okay. But Rock..." Her voice failed as she pictured him on the floor again, blood soaking his clothes. "There was so much blood, Jake. What if the paramedics didn't get to him in time? If he dies, it's my fault."

"He's where he needs to be. The doctors here are excellent."

Using her palm, she wiped the tears from her cheek. "I know, but I'm scared." Reluctantly, she moved out of Jake's embrace and went for the tissue box. "What's taking so long?" She wiped her nose and eyes before noticing her cousin's shirt. She'd drenched a large section of it. "I'm sorry. I didn't intend to give you a bath."

In true Jake fashion, he gave her a nonchalant shrug. "Don't worry about it. Garret does worse after each feeding. Have you heard anything?"

"Nope. Shouldn't they have some kind of update?"

Grabbing the tissue box and her hand, he led her over to the cheap sofa. "Sit. When they have an update, they'll tell us." He plucked out several clean tissues and shoved them in her hand. "Did you call his family?"

"I tried his parents. They didn't answer." She'd been more than a little relieved when the call went to voicemail. She'd rather talk to them when she could tell them Rock was okay. Or even better, let Rock call and tell them himself. Unfortunately, she recognized the possibility that she might have to tell them the exact opposite. "Addie went into labor tonight. Actually, I guess it was last night." Allison lost track of time but knew it was now sometime early Saturday morning. "Rock's parents went to the hospital to be with her and Trent. Since they didn't answer, I guess they're still with them."

"I didn't know Addie went into labor. Trent didn't call me. What about Rock's brothers? Did you try any of them?"

"No. I don't have their numbers. I only have Marta's because I helped her plan Addie's bridal shower." What a lifetime ago the event seemed. "And I can't call Addie and ask her for them."

"It's possible the police have informed them already anyway. They must have procedures for handling situations like this."

Stupid, stupid. She should've realized the police would inform his parents. When the police officers questioned her, they asked about Rock's family. Why else would they ask if they didn't plan on contacting them? "I gave them his parents' names and address. But if they're still with Addie, the police might not have reached them yet either." She didn't know which would be worse, getting news your son had been shot from a police officer or from someone who loved him.

Again, the waiting room door opened. A tall, lanky man perhaps in his early fifties with wire-rimmed glasses and dressed in hospital scrubs entered. His expression remained neutral.

Please tell me good news, Allison prayed, wringing her hands together.

Jake stood and shook the doctor's hand. "Bradley," he greeted. "Allison, this is Dr. Bradley Ford," Jake explained before speaking to the doctor again. "How's he doing?"

Okay, Jake knew the doctor. Fabulous, now get on with it.

"Jake, Miss Sherbrooke." The doctor extended his hand in

her direction before he sat. "Rocco's out of surgery and in stable condition. He's lucky. Neither bullet struck any vital organs. The bullet to his thigh passed straight through muscle and missed the femur. Both injuries could have been much worse."

Stable condition. She heard what she considered the most important part of the sentence and couldn't control the sound that escaped. It wasn't one of gut-wrenching sobs like earlier, but more of a strangled gasp.

"Is something wrong, Miss Sherbrooke?" Dr. Ford paused in his explanation of Rock's injuries.

"Allison." Jake put his arm around her shoulder and gave them a squeeze. "It's good news."

"He's going to be okay?" She knew stable condition didn't always equal a successful recovery. Complications could creep up and cause unexpected outcomes.

The doctor's neutral expression faded and a more compassionate one replaced it. "Some risk comes with any surgery. However, he's healthy and young. I expect him to make a full recovery."

"Can I see him?"

"Once he's moved and settled into a room, you can visit. In the meantime, try to relax. Maybe go downstairs for a tea or a snack. It might be a while before you can go up."

Relax? The doctor's surgical cap must be too tight or something if he thought she could relax. Maybe after she saw Rock, she'd relax, but not until then. "Thank you, but I'll wait here."

Dr. Ford looked at Jake, who still held her hand. "Don't worry, Bradley. I'll stay with her and make sure she gets whatever she needs."

"Excellent. I'll have someone inform you both when he's settled and ready for visitors."

When the door closed behind the doctor, Allison sagged back against the sofa. Rock was alive. He'd be in pain when he woke up, but he would wake up.

"Can I get you anything?"

"No thanks, Jake. The only thing I need is to see him."

Jake leaned back next to her. "You heard Bradley. It could be awhile. You look exhausted. Some coffee might help you stay awake."

Starting at the moment her doorknob rattled, adrenaline and fear kept her body going. With both those things gone, exhaustion was settling in. "Maybe coffee's a good idea. Make it the biggest they have. Put some sugar in it too. Maybe it'll give me an extra little boost."

"You've got it. Be right back. Call me if you want anything else."

He started for the door. Allison's ringing smartphone stopped him.

She'd shoved the device and her keys in her jeans pocket when she'd rushed out the door. Now she pulled it out and checked the screen. *Trent.* Was he calling with an update on Addie? She hadn't received any updates from him or her dad, but would he call this late? Trent would want to share the news, but considering the time, she suspected he'd wait until a more acceptable hour. If not about the baby, he had only one other reason to call now. The police had informed Marta and Sal of what happened and they'd passed the information on to him. She'd never get out of telling her family everything, but she'd prefer to do it much later. Perhaps after she saw Rock and got a little rest.

"Are you going to answer the phone?" Jake asked.

"It's Trent."

"Do you want me to answer?"

"No, I got it." Letting Jake answer would only postpone the inevitable. At least now she could tell Trent they were both alive and safe. "Hello," she said.

"Where are you? What the hell is going on?" Trent didn't pause so she could answer before he continued. "Are you okay? Marta called me, hysterical. She said Rock was rushed to the hospital after being shot. I sent a car to drive her and Sal to the airport. Dad's plane is waiting for them. The police didn't have an update on his condition."

When Trent stopped for a breath, she jumped in. "I'm fine and in a waiting room at the hospital. Jake is with me. Have you told anyone else?" No matter what, her dad and the rest of her family would worry, but perhaps they'd worry less if they knew she was okay.

"Thank God." She heard him blow out a deep breath. "Only Dad and Abby. I needed to check on you before I called anyone else. And I didn't want to tell Addie anything about Rock until I knew more."

"He's out of surgery and in stable condition. The doctor said the bullets didn't hit any vital organs. I'm waiting to go up and see him."

"That's excellent news. But what the hell happened down there? Were you with him?"

"I'll tell you everything later. I promise. Right now, can we just leave it at I'm okay and Rock will recover?" Telling her brother would mean reliving the night. She didn't have it in her right now.

"You're not hurt?"

"Honest. I don't have a scratch on me. Rock made sure I stayed safe."

Trent huffed. The protective big brother in him wanted all the answers tonight. "Okay, I'll wait for the whole story. Call me when you get home and keep me updated on how Rock is doing. I need to call Marta before the plane leaves so they know Rock's stable. She was a wreck when I talked to her."

She pictured the puddles of blood on her bedroom floor. She wasn't sure she could ever sleep in there again. "Wait." She needed some happy news. The birth of a baby qualified. "How's Addie. Did she have the baby yet?" She'd lost track of how many hours ago her dad announced Addie started labor, but it sure seemed like a long time.

"Addie's beat and the baby is asleep."

Finally, she had something positive to focus on while she waited. "Well, do I have a niece or a nephew?"

"Nephew. Kendrick was born two and half hours ago. I'll send you pictures later this morning. When you see Rock, tell him the news. I need to go."

She understood Trent's urgency. Once she received word on Rock's condition, she should have tried Marta again herself. Rock's parents deserved to know what was happening. However, she was pleased she didn't have to do it. At some point, she'd have to talk to them, but right now she didn't want to admit to them their son had almost died because of her.

"Did Addie have a boy or a girl?" Jake asked when she put the phone away. He'd moved closer while she spoke to her brother. Allison suspected Jake wanted Trent's firstborn to be a boy too. Growing up, he and Trent had been like brothers. Less than a year apart in age, they'd been inseparable growing up until they'd gone to different universities. She could picture her cousin wanting his son, Garret, to have a similar relationship with his cousins.

"A boy. I'm sure James, Garret, and Kendrick will get into all kinds of trouble together," she said, referring to Jake's nephew who'd been born in the fall.

"Never," Jake said and winked. "They'll be well-behaved gentleman like Trent and me."

From somewhere deep inside, laughter rolled up and over her and it took her several seconds to get it under control. "I needed that. Thank you."

"Glad I could help. Do you still want coffee?"

Allison wiped the tears from her eyes, glad they were now tears from laughing instead of crying. "Please. Marta and Sal are on their way. I'm going to try to stay until they get here."

FOG FILLED his head and cotton coated his mouth. Rock ignored both and opened his eyes. Sterile white walls and a small television mounted a few inches from the ceiling greeted him. A tidal wave of memories rushed back. Allison's stalker had gotten in the house. The bastard had been so close to harming her. When he'd seen the guy standing in her doorway, absolute fear had gripped him. Fear like nothing he'd every experienced before or wanted to again.

Where was she now? What about her stalker? Hunter, he'd heard Allison call him. He'd gone for the SOB's carotid artery. Often, that kind of injury killed a man. He hoped it had tonight. Hunter deserved death for the hell he'd put Allison through.

He tried moving in bed, but everything felt sluggish. *Damn anesthesia.* He hated the stuff. Took forever for it to wear off completely. Rock shifted his upper body again and winced at the pull in his side. He didn't need to look. He remembered the shots Hunter got off. He wasn't looking forward to when the pain meds wore off.

"You're awake." Allison walked in the room. She appeared pale and her hair looked like it hadn't seen a brush in days, but she was walking and talking.

"If ya can call it awake. My head's in the clouds." He rubbed his forehead and watched her come closer. "How long have you been here?"

"Since the ambulance brought you in. But they just let me come up to your room." She dropped a featherlight kiss on his lips before she pulled a chair over. "Your mom and dad are on their way."

"Mannaggia."

"I don't know what that means, but I'm guessing you're not happy they're coming."

"There's no need for them to waste the money. I'm fine. You really didn't need to call them."

"When I called, they didn't answer. The Providence police actually told them. And then Trent sent them down on dad's jet. They should be here soon." Allison took his hand. "But they needed to know, Rock. If the police hadn't told them, I would have kept trying until I got them."

"Mom doesn't handle this kind of news well. She's a tough woman; you'd think she would, but it's just the opposite." Any other crisis and his mom took control, but when it came to sick or injured family members, she fell apart.

"At least she knows you're okay. Trent called and I filled him in on your condition. He passed the info on to your parents."

It would help, but he'd still face some serious fussing over him. And he'd suck it up and deal with it like he'd done in the past. After all, it was his mom. "A doctor hasn't been in yet. What did they tell ya?"

"Dr. Ford said the bullets didn't hit any organs and that the one through your thigh missed the femur and the artery."

Considering the fact he was awake and they were talking, he'd assumed the bullets hadn't caused any life threatening injuries. Now on to more important matters. "Are you okay?" He recalled asking her the same question after his fight with Hunter and she answered yes. Honestly, he didn't know if he'd actually asked or just dreamed he did.

She rolled her lips together and looked away for a moment. "He didn't hurt me." Her voice quivered a little. "I'm still shaken up though. And in shock. Hunter is Charles's younger brother. He's a junior at Georgetown University. He plays football and was talking about summer internships in my office. I just don't understand."

She kept referring to him in the present tense. He hoped the creep hadn't lived. "Did he make it?"

"No, he was gone when the paramedics got there."

What a shame.

"Maybe if I'd done something, he would've lived. I didn't even try." She sounded guilty, which angered him. Nothing had been her fault. "This sounds horrible, but I didn't care. You needed me; that was all that mattered."

"It's not horrible, Ally." Man, he wanted to wrap his arms

around her and make the entire hellish night disappear. "I would've done the same. The scumbag got what he deserved."

"I know." Tears pooled in her eyes and he knew she'd lose the battle of holding them back soon.

"Everything's over. You're safe."

She choked back a sob and nodded, causing her hair to fall forward. "I was so scared you weren't going to make it. Blood was everywhere and you got so pale." She pushed her hair back behind her ears, revealing the tears that fell down her face. "I love you, and the idea of losing you—"

"Ya didn't. I'm here. You're here. Everything's fine." He tried to sit up more, but the pain slowly inching its way through his body stopped him.

"You're in pain, aren't you?"

So much for not wincing. "Not too bad. Pain meds are just starting to wear off. Must be almost time for more." This wasn't the first time he'd suffered a gunshot wound. He knew the drill. Rather than focus on his condition or what she'd experienced, he changed the subject. "Did Addie have the baby?"

"Yep, earlier this morning. A little boy. They named him Kendrick. Trent promised to send pictures later today." A little sadness remained in her voice, but she sounded much more like herself.

"Sweet, I won the bet."

"What bet?"

"With Jon and Frank. They insisted she was having a girl," he answered, referring to his older brothers. "We couldn't get in touch with Tom to include him."

"Trent must be on cloud nine. I can't wait to see the baby."

He was close to that himself and he wasn't even the father. He could only imagine how his brother-in-law and sister felt. "Go tomorrow. Spend a few days up there. You deserve a few days away after last night." With her stalker dead, she had her freedom back. She could visit Providence or anywhere else before getting back into her normal routine again.

"Not with you in here. When you get out and can travel, we'll go together like we planned."

He didn't consider himself a super emotional guy, but damn if he didn't like her answer. "I love you. And when I get outta here, I plan on taking my time and showing you just how much."

"I'm holding you to that." She smiled for the first time since coming in. "And looking forward to it," she added, standing up and giving him a peck on the lips.

"Not so fast," he said when she tried to move away. With her so close, he planned on kissing her right. Rock brought her mouth toward his. "That wasn't a kiss," he whispered before he devoured her lips and showed her what a real kiss was.

The throat clearing got his attention. *Damn it.* Someone had come in the room. Rock let his lips linger a moment longer before he pulled away. His parents stood inside the room, the door again closing behind them. His mom looked like death warmed over, as she'd say. Her clothes were rumpled, her eyes red, and she had on two different shoes. His dad, who'd done the throat clearing, looked the same as always. No matter the situation, he appeared calm and in charge.

"He looks fine to me," his dad said as they approached the bed.

Color climbed Allison's face, but she faced his parents. "Hi, Marta, Sal. Maybe I should give you some time alone."

He'd prefer if she stayed, but she looked ready to fall asleep on the spot. She needed sleep, not a visit with him and his parents.

"Jake invited me to stay with him. I'll get some rest and come back in a few hours."

Considering the state of her house, bunking with her cousin made sense. "No rush. I'm not going anywhere."

"You might want to wait. Mark and Abby will be up in a minute. He got a phone call as we walked in the hospital," his mom said.

"They're here too?"

His mom appeared surprised by the question. "We all flew down together. I thought you knew we were all coming."

Mark Sherbrooke entered the room, his wife a step or two behind him. With the exception of the missing tie, he wore the same clothes as when they'd met for dinner the night before. Like Allison and his mom, Mark had the walking dead look going on. His wife only looked slightly better.

"Dad, Abby, you didn't need to come." Her words came out muffled as Mark enveloped her in a hug. "I'm fine."

Tears glistened in his eyes when he pulled away. "Of course I did." The guy sounded like he'd drank a glass of sand on the trip down.

Rock could only imagine the wide range of emotions the guy had experienced tonight. Actually, the same went for his parents.

"How are you, Rock?" Mark turned his attention on him, which apparently was a cue for everyone to look in his direction.

"Fine, sir." His leg and side throbbed and he knew it'd only get worse as the pain meds continued to wear off. He'd never admit it.

"Mark, remember?" He put his arm around Allison's shoulders. Judging by his expression, he didn't intend to let her go anytime soon. "If you need anything, let me know."

The man had his arm around the only thing he needed. "Thank you."

"Marta, Sal, we'll wait down the hall so you can visit with Rock alone. Just come and get us when you're ready to leave."

He appreciated that they'd come down, but at the moment, he'd prefer if everyone but Allison left. Telling his mom he didn't want her there was not an option. Dropping a hint or two was something else. "Come back later, Mom. You and Dad spent all night at the hospital with Addie. Get some sleep. It's my plan."

"Mine too," Allison chimed in, either because she wanted to leave or she understood his intention.

His mom frowned, torn between staying and getting sleep.

"When you get back, I'll be right here."

"I imagine everyone here could use some rest. When I come back, I want to know exactly what happened," his mom said with some reluctance.

"Get some rest. We'll see you in a few," his dad said, clapping him on the shoulder.

His parents and Abby headed for the door, leaving Allison and Mark behind. "Why don't you stay with us tonight," Mark said, his arm still firmly around her shoulders.

Allison did a perfect imitation of a deer in headlights and licked her bottom lip. "Jake invited me to stay with him."

"Oh, then we can drop you off there on the way to the hotel." Despite his obvious disappointment, he didn't argue. "I know you want a minute alone. I'll wait outside with everyone." He kissed her cheek and left to join his wife and Rock's parents.

"I like him," Rock said.

"Told you so." Taking his hand, she kissed his bruised knuckles. "I hate to leave, but you need rest and I'm beat. And I'm going to need all the energy I can get. Dad's going to want the entire story. Do you need anything before I go?"

More pain meds and some sleep in that order. "All good."

"Be back soon. I love you." She leaned over and gave him a gentle kiss.

"Love ya too." He hated watching her leave, but at least she was safe. He'd protected her from harm. She could walk around and not worry someone followed her. Assuming she'd have him, he planned to spend the rest of his life protecting her.

I'm looking forward to a hospital visit. There's something wrong with that. Over the past two days, it seemed the hospital was the only place she got any privacy. If it wasn't one of her relatives visiting her at Jake's house, one of them was calling to check on her. She appreciated their concern, but she needed them all to back off. Her family wasn't the worst of it though. When the media got wind of what happened, they descended on her. They called her phone. They camped outside the entrance to Jake's gated community. A few even tried to get into Rock's hospital room for an interview. Thankfully, the security guard her dad had stationed outside the door sent them packing.

Even though the media hadn't spoken to her or Rock directly, it hadn't stopped them from running various stories. A few had gotten most of the facts correct, but a handful had been pure fiction. One even claimed she and Hunter had been in a relationship and he lost it when he discovered her and Rock together. Then there had been the stories about Hunter. They'd painted him as a college student with a bright and promising future who'd snapped. While she didn't mourn Hunter, she felt sympathy toward his family. Charles and his brother had been close, and losing a child, no matter their age, must be difficult. Charles had even called her, but she didn't answer. What could she say to him? His brother had tried to kill her and Rock. He'd come close to succeeding. Maybe in the distant future, she could carry on a conversation, but not now.

"Good afternoon, Miss Sherbrooke," the guard outside Rock's room said when she approached.

"Hello, Kent. Any more reporters today?"

"Nice and quiet so far."

She hoped it stayed quiet.

The scent of fried food hit her when she walked inside. A tray of untouched mashed potatoes with some congealed gravy over them and what vaguely resembled meatloaf rested on a chair. In bed, Rock worked his way through a large burger. The takeout box in front of him was overflowing with onion rings, and a large soft drink completed the meal. "I was going to go out and get whatever you wanted. Looks like you're all set."

His dark eyes swung in her direction. "Connor brought this with him. He left about fifteen minutes ago. Help yourself." He indicated toward the box. "This is my second burger. I wish he'd brought a beer too."

Eating food from outside the hospital was one thing. Drinking alcohol while confined to a bed and getting pain medication was another. "I'm glad he didn't. Anyone else visit?" He'd had numerous visitors from the base. So many at times she'd left the small room due to the amount of male testosterone floating around.

"Eric Coleman came with him. He wanted an answer about the job with the firm."

"Seriously? What a creep. He wanted an answer while you're sitting in a hospital bed with gunshot wounds?"

"Coleman has his reasons. But it doesn't matter. I told him no."

"Then when I start looking for a new house, I'll look for one closer to you and the base."

He didn't look surprised by her announcement. In fact, he looked like he expected her to say she planned to move out of her current townhouse. "Don't bother. Come live with me. It's small, but when my lease is up, we can look for something you like better."

She'd hoped he'd suggest they get a place together. "I'd love to. Do you think Baxter will mind?" The dog had been moping, if a dog could mope anyway, around Jake's house since he got there. She'd considered trying to sneak him in the hospital for a visit.

"Nah, he likes ya. Give him a few extra treats everyday and he'll be your best friend."

Rock cleared his throat and seriousness oozed from his body. Whatever he intended to say, she wasn't going to like.

"Doc says the leg will take a while to heal. I won't be leaving in June as planned. Doesn't mean I won't deploy again."

"I know." She'd asked the doctor about Rock's injuries and what his recovery would look like.

"In a year or two, I planned on applying to one of the

government agencies and seeing what happened. Maybe FBI or DEA. It'd give me more freedom. Less time away from family. Can ya handle my life the way it is until then?"

She'd grown up having everything she wanted and the freedom to go wherever she wished. She'd never considered having it any other way. If being with Rock meant she needed to make a few sacrifices, she would. "Looks like we'll be getting a lot of visits from my family." If she and Rock couldn't visit Providence as often as her dad liked, he'd be making a lot of trips south.

"You're sure?"

Men. "Positive." Then, just in case he still didn't believe her, she used her mouth to convince him.

CHAPTER 22

FIVE WEEKS later

HE'D LOVE to start a fire and toss his crutches in it. Rock eased himself down and leaned the offending objects against a table. He was damn sick of the things. When he did get rid of them, he had a wonderful cane to look forward to. People told him how lucky he'd been. He couldn't deny it and he reminded himself often. He was also thankful he'd ended up hurt and not Allison. Events that night could have turned out so much differently.

He'd quickly come to terms with his actions that night. He'd done what he had to. Protecting Allison had been all that mattered. She struggled with what happened. The first week or so after the attack, she had nightmares every night. Allison assured him they had stopped and he believed her. She no longer called out in her sleep or woke up drenched in sweat. She still visited a therapist, and he guessed those sessions were doing the trick. Looking at her across the room laughing with her brother Gray and his fiancée, no one would ever suspect what she'd gone through.

"Do you want to hold him?" Addie sat down next to him, Kendrick in her arms.

Tonight had been the first time he'd seen his nephew. As much as he'd wanted to fly up sooner, he'd been in too much pain. Even the trip up for Sara's wedding, which was tomorrow, had been unpleasant, but he'd known how important it was to Allison.

"He's fed and changed, so he's good for a little bit."

Kendrick had spent the night so far either being held by one of the many Sherbrookes in the room or sleeping. "What do I need to do?" He'd never held an infant, and the little guy was so tiny.

Addie passed his nephew to him. "It's not complicated. Just be sure to support his neck."

Dark blue eyes gazed back up at him, instantly grabbing a hold of his heart. "How are you doing?" he asked. Over the past several weeks, he'd spoken only a handful of times with his sister.

"I should be asking you."

"Gettin' better. Should be ready for a cane soon."

"And how's Allison?" Addie lowered her voice when she asked the question.

Mesmerized by the bundle in his arms, he kept his gaze on his nephew. "Okay."

"She looks happy."

Rock looked up and in Allison's direction. She'd finished up her convo with Gray and was headed toward him. The sight brought an automatic smile to his face.

"You're in *love*," Addie teased.

Damn right. "Yep."

"The feeling is mutual."

He didn't need his sister to tell him Allison loved him. She both told him and showed him everyday.

"I know."

Allison took the spot on the other side of him. "Know what? That it's my turn to hold my nephew."

"I love you, but you're not getting him."

"Should I go find an egg timer and set it so you can take turns?" Addie asked.

"Hilarious."

"But not a bad idea," Allison added, giving him an overly bright smile.

"Considering Derek's headed this way, we might need it." Addie nodded across the room. "He's been in an odd mood since last month. Hope he left it at home tonight."

"I noticed the same thing when he's called." Even though Rock still held the baby, Allison reached out and touched his little hand. "I thought maybe it was my imagination."

"Nope. Ever since your aunt convinced him to take part in the bachelor auction, he's been in not so much a bad mood, but not himself either."

"What auction?"

His sister smiled, surprised she knew something Allison didn't. "The foundation is holding a bachelor auction next weekend. Your Aunt Marilyn strong-armed Derek and your cousin Scott into taking part."

"You're kidding. A bachelor auction?"

Rock had a similar thought himself. Followed by, better Derek than him.

"Who came up with the idea of an auction? Not my aunt."

"Rose, your replacement. At first, Marilyn was against it, but Rose won her over. So far, it's been a success. Almost all the tickets have been sold."

"I might come back just for that." Allison nudged him on his good side and smiled at him. "My turn. Hand over my nephew."

Damn, when she smiled at him like that, he couldn't deny her anything. "Only because I love you," he whispered in her ear before handing the baby off to her.

"Love you too, and I'll reward you later. Promise."
The End

To READ Derek's story pick up *Bidding on the Billionaire* book 8 in the Sherbrookes of Newport.

OTHER BOOKS BY CHRISTINA

*Loving the Billionaire, a novella

*The Teacher's Billionaire, book 1

*The Billionaire Playboy, book 2

*The Billionaire Princess, book 3

*The Billionaire's Best Friend, book 4

*Redeeming the Billionaire, book 5

*More Than a Billionaire, book 6

*Protecting the Billionaire, book 7

*Bidding on the Billionaire, book 8

*Falling for the Billionaire, book 9

*The Billionaire Next Door, book 10

*The Billionaire's Homecoming, book 11

+The Courage to Love, book 1

+Hometown Love, book 2

+The Playboy Next Door, book 3

+In Hiss Kiss, book 4

+A Promise To Keep, book 5

^Born To Protect

*The Sherbrookes of Newport series
+Love on the North Shore series
^Elite Force Security series

ABOUT CHRISTINA TETREAULT

USA Today best selling author Christina Tetreault started writing at the age of ten on her grandmother's manual typewriter and never stopped. Born and raised in Lincoln, Rhode Island, she has lived in four of the six New England states since getting married in 2001. Today, she lives in New Hampshire with her husband, three daughters, and two dogs. When she is not driving her daughters around to their various activities or chasing around the dogs, she is working on a story or reading a romance novel. Currently, she has two series out, The Sherbrookes of Newport and Love on the North Shore. She plans to release a third in the summer. You can visit her website www.christinatetreault.com or follow her on Facebook to learn more about her characters and to track her progress on current writing projects.

Made in the USA
Las Vegas, NV
06 May 2022

48467108R00125